AND THEN

THERE ARE THE STORIES

Some other books by the same author:

The Ubuntu Tradition in the White Cat Books
(Amazon 2023)

White Cat – a not entirely fictional mystery
(Amazon 2022)

Just Be Here – the guide to musicking mindfulness
(Amazon, 2020)

Essentials for Living in a Troubled World – contemplations and meditations for survival in our testing times
(Amazon 2020)

Pathways – humanity's search for its soul
(Amazon, 2017, 2019)

Stillness in Mind – a companion to mindfulness, meditation, living
(Changemakers Books, 2014)

AND THEN

THERE ARE THE STORIES

a sequel to **White Cat**

by

SIMON COLE

White Cat

Books

for Janet

from the author's journal…

I wondered whether these things were such that they should be written down, or whether it was better they were left to be covered over by the sands of time. What do the deeds of we humans matter once the players themselves and the witnesses to their deeds are all dead? Or does their play go on despite that? Even in the remembering is someone affected? Our lives in fact a continuous thread ceaselessly spun from inexhaustible staple?

At the start I knew Barbara, and I had known Louie. Soon there were others, and Hugh appeared – I could have known Hugh, but in the end I did not, though I have a photograph. I had known about Harry, long gone of course, but in a way the source of all this. And then Nobomi – her name means life, mother of life, source of being – Nobomi was everywhere, Turangalila.

Hugh was damaged, and that is how you meet him here, but so was Nobomi – life is never invulnerable to itself – and the daughter's agony is the mother's tragedy, the mother's agony the daughter's destruction.

Hugh, Nobomi, they travel together to the place where their paths separate and they find resolution in a mutual resignation. Ubuntu was their code… the thread could go on spinning.

There was another… and the thread still goes on spinning.

part one

"There is sex and death and then there are the stories,
Eros and Thanatos are mute until the storytellers come..."

from 'Counterpoint' by Petrūska Clarkson

"This isn't right. Where's Barbara?"

"Who is Barbara?"

"You can't be Barbara, you're black."

"There's no-one else here, Hugh."

"How do you know my name?"

"You tell me. Every time you came, you always told me."

"Every time I came? But who are you?"

"I don't tell you. I don't speak."

"You are speaking."

"Now, but not then."

"It should have been Barbara... we are going to have tea... in Bath... You're not... Have I seen you before?"

"Many times."

"Who are you?"

"I am Nobomi."

"Nobomi. I've heard Nobomi. Somewhere... and Harry. Where is Harry?"

"I don't know Harry. Who is he?"

"I don't know. They keep on asking me, but I don't know. Every time they want to know – who is Harry? I tell them I don't know, I don't know, I don't know. But they don't stop. They scream at me. Every time and..."

"Nobomi... Nobomi... Will you stay?"

"Yes, I am staying, Hugh."

He fell asleep.

It happened often, that he appeared to wake up in a dream, no, it was more like a nightmare. She did not understand what it was, even though she might have guessed where it came from. But she just waited.

She knew that she had her own evil spirit.

a sighting, not the first...

Bathandwa

I can't remember how long it was before I realised that they had always been there, somewhere over there on the veldt, where it starts to rise, far beyond the deep valley the river cuts. Of course, the river is still a long way off, but you lose all sense of scale with the Drakensberg. It sits there massive and forbidding in the distance. My ancestors thought it was the wall at the end of the world. Dragon's mountain, that's Drakensberg, but they called it uKhahlamba, the wall of spears.

You might look out across the veldt at that end of the world for your whole life and see nothing moving, my father used to say. Its presence – the *intaba* and its skirt, he said – it's like it draws everything into itself and gives back nothing.

So there I was, I had been grazing my cattle most of that summer season, slowly moving them across the plain eastwards, the dragon's wall looming up alongside me. I had come a long way before I even realised they were over there. At first they had been so far away I could not even tell whether they were on foot or on horseback. But no, they were riding. They were on the course grass slopes below that bare rocky outcrop there, that breaks away from the far side of the plain. It looks like it's a miniature of the great monster looming above it. They were scarcely more than dots from this distance, those two, so it didn't surprise me that I hadn't seen them before. Why today? Why did they appear today? Maybe it was because of the angle of the light on the sloping hillside. You notice that when you're around here a long time – the hills, the crags, they look completely different depending on the light. Can catch you out sometimes. From over here you couldn't really make out movement, except that if you looked away for a few minutes and then looked back you might notice the dots lined up with a different bit of the outcrop behind.

With these two, though, what puzzled me was they seemed to be going even slower than me and I was walking behind grazing cows. So slow, that in a few days I would leave 'em behind. I couldn't work out why this took up my thoughts so much, except there's not too much to think about up here. That and wondering where they'd have come from. Not where they were heading – somewhere over on that hillside was a track which ended up in Matatiele – never'd gone that way myself but I'd seen where it arrived in all the homesteads and kraals that made up that place. No, not where they were heading, but where they might've come from, because there's no obvious place two travellers would've set off from for a hundred miles or more back along the mountainside. I could see there were two of them and I could also see that sometimes there was a distance between them, but other times they merged into one. Sometimes, as well, they'd moved when you looked back, but other times they appeared to be in the same place.

You'll be wondering why I didn't go over to them. You'll be thinking, if there are so few people on the veldt, does your heart not yearn for human company and jump at any chance of it, if you are on your own? But you cannot understand the distances between people here in those times. Not just physical distance. Of course there was always that out here. You probably thought from my description that it would be like taking the path to the hill on the other side of the valley, like in your country. No, it's not like that here. I cannot tell you what the distance was, because miles don't mean much to me, but it would have been more than a day's journey. And that's not all, because between people there was another kind of separation in those years: we had to keep in our own places then, or at least, *we* did, Blacks and Coloureds. And you were never sure about people you didn't know. Safer with your own kind. We got used to that.

Course, I wondered who they were. In my life I had a lot of time to wonder. I was curious – were they two men – that's most likely – or a man and a woman? Were they Xhosa or Sotho or Zulu? Less likely they would be Afrikaners, but they could be Boers. Two Europeans would not be very likely up here, but it could be a white man and a black girl. This is silly speculation. I'll most likely never know. Look how your mind wanders along all sorts of pathways when you are on your own without any human company. But one thing I realised was – black, white, man, woman, African, European – those weren't things that you could tell from this distance, no, you just saw two people living through their own stuff, whatever that was. I suppose that's how 'tis – we mostly live our lives in parallel, we mostly never know what's happening for other people, even if it's happening right alongside. We might see what they're doing, but we've no idea what it's about.

I remember something my father told me. When he was about 18, he told me, he had gone to the big town down by the Ocean, called East London, but we called it eMonti. My father did tell me lots of things, and I think this one he was telling me was warning me. He used to go to a place of drinking alcohol near the sea shore. Most of them were Xhosa who went there, young, some girls, but many were kids like him. He said a white boy used to come in every Friday on his own and then he started coming in with a Xhosa girl. You saw that sort of thing, a white boy walking with a native girl, but not often you saw them going to a place of drinking alcohol of black people. It was at the time the segregation was starting, about 1900, the council making regulations, but people in that part of town were not yet noticing much. These two were accepted because the boy was different from other white boys, he had a regular job, but he was an easy sort, mixed in, no airs. My father even remembered his name, Harry, but he didn't know the girl's name, even though she was Xhosa like him. He always wondered about them, he couldn't understand them. He said the girl was always looking round, as if she were afraid, didn't speak to anyone even though we's mostly her own kind, it was her boy was talking, Harry. But they heard a few things, them talking together, they could tell she didn't come from the town, even thought she might have come from up this way, and this is a very long way from eMonti. My father said there were stories that were told. Some people said he had a hold over her because he knew many people, some said she was a prostitute, but it wasn't likely a white man using a black girl would take her into a place of drinking alcohol of Xhosa people, some thought he had got her pregnant and was trying to find a Xhosa boy to smear him. Then it all changed and suddenly *she* was the one who was happy and he wasn't easy and casual any longer, he went very quiet. Then they just stopped coming. Two weeks later this Harry was found dead on the beach. He had drowned. No-one ever saw the girl again. No-one even knew her name.

"They stayed in my mind," my father said – "I was just going along, everything ordinary, and right next to me there was some big tragedy about to happen."

. . .

They've gone. I don't see them any more. I've been helping a limping calf all morning – it'd panicked when it saw a snake, tried to clamber up some rocks and got a sharp stone wedged deep between its hooves. I just finished and looked up and they were not there any longer. It could be they've gone behind where the veldt rises, or they might have gone down to the river, but it's dangerous that way. Me, I would keep to the track, the valley sides are steep and treacherous. Horses don't like it much down in there.

I'll get to Matatiele in a few days. I know a few folks there and I'm staying for a while with my brother, so I think I will ask and see if they arrived there. It's a very scattered place, but no-one comes into these upland regions without being seen by someone. Of course, I don't know who I'm asking after, just two travellers on horseback. But there are still a lot of horses up here, so it's likely someone will have seen them.

hope pending…

Eva

We should have been used to situations changing quickly in those days. If you were running a hostel for homeless girls in the middle of an unstable city, as it was then, all the time you could have arrivals and departures, no, we should really call them appearances and disappearances. Which is why we had a strict time for shutting the doors at the end of the day – 7 in winter and 9 in summer. Then you counted how many residents and overnights you had. And you counted again in the morning. Not that the doors were ever left unlocked, it was just the latest time for a new arrival. Security? It shouldn't have been such a headache, but in Vienna after the war you could not trust anyone. Infiltrators, agents, informers everywhere. You couldn't even be sure of a uniform completely. We had a kind of hierarchy of trustworthiness for uniforms. Safest were the armies – British, French, American – in that order – the Russians didn't even get on the list. Then the Bundespolizei and after them the Gemeindewachkörper, but private militias could appear in uniform as well and then there were the State Secret Police which could plant informers – domestics were a favourite – and we were especially vulnerable there.

You always hoped you didn't need to question people's honesty like – whether it was the ones who brought the girls in, or the ones that came round all official with papers and photos and said they were on an investigation and had to speak to this or that girl – but they had so many photos, them, I think they had gone round the streets snapping. We lost a few that way. But the worst was when you had been really sure of someone and everything goes well, for the girl as well, and then, some'ow, it all seems to go wrong. And you want to believe you weren't taken in, that they were really ok, and something sudden and desperate or nasty 'adn't happened – it was like that often enough in this city. For perfectly innocent people as well. I remember one time in particular. I'd opened the door and let them in the first time so I felt sort of responsible. I don't have Frau Winkel's stern face – we used to think she probably discouraged at least half of the doubtful callers before they even got over the doormat. My weakness, I suppose, I smile too much. But then he did as well – Hugh, that was his name, British army, officer, smart of course, always were, very grateful to find us open, very polite, apologising that it was late – it wasn't – and what should he do? Something slightly odd, though, one of those things you notice and think, oh it's not really important, but you've noticed it, and then things move on and you forget. I'll tell you what it was... I asked him for his ID – always seems a bit silly for an officer in uniform like that, but we have to do it – and he must 'ave heard me, but he got on talking about something and then when I started to ask him again, he started up on something else, and then things moved on and I never asked him again, so he never showed me. He wouldn't have got away with that if it had been Frau Winkel.

But this Hugh had a girl of about 14 with him, said he had found her in Stephansplatz, she had run into his arms when a wall fell down – I hadn't heard about it, though I do remember some commotion not long before. Anyway could we give her a safe lodging, because he had seen her before and she never seemed to be with anyone and looked like she was homeless? So I said we could and started on filling in the form, and straightaway I ran into a problem. The girls weren't allowed to wear no jewellery, we listed it and keep valuables locked up so that there was no thieving, but this girl had a gold locket and the officer said she was inseparable from it, he thought if we tried to take it away she would just turn round and run. I had to talk to the warden, the officer did too, and after a lot of discussion she's allowed to keep it. Mind she never lost it all the time she was with us. Could have been because she had one hand round it every time you saw her! But it might also 'ave been because the other girls were always very cautious of her, and that was probably to do with her being different. I think they was probably a bit scared too. I didn't say, did I? She was black, well, very dark brown, like. And she seemed to go around in her own world. The only other person in that world was this Hugh. It was lucky, him being an army officer, we said he could come back and check on her if he wanted. And he did, most every day. It got so that she knew when he was going to arrive, usually in the afternoon, and she would come down to the reception place we have near the entrance and sit facing the door looking at a book, and when he arrived she got up and walked towards him smiling, and then together they would go up to the gallery on the third floor and sit side by side looking out of the big window over the city. I never saw him touch her, not even a hand on her shoulder like, and I never saw them talking. They just sat silently. He would always say to her when he arrived, "Hello, my name is Hugh", but she said nothing. She said nothing to nobody, 'til the last day he came.

There seemed to be something different 'bout that day, even before it happened. Being the last, I mean.

Hugh arrived much earlier than usual. He hadn't come for a couple of days, but she seemed to know he was going to come that day and she was there waiting for him in the usual way. She stood up and walked across and he said, as always, "Hello, my name is Hugh" and, for the very first time, she answered 'im, "I am Nobomi". Then she took his

hand and they walked together to their usual place, lookin'
out over the city. Most of the time they sat silently
together as they always did, but that day I did see her
show him her locket. But when he left, she didn't walk
with him to the door. On the way out he said to us, "Her
name is Nobomi. She speaks a very little English, but I
don't know how she came to Vienna. She said her white
cat Umzuli wandered away. I don't know when I shall be
able to see her again. I have told her that, but I cannot tell
whether she understood me. Please give her whatever help
you can, but if there is something more you need, here is
an address," and he handed me a piece of paper which said
– Barbara, Cleeve Hill Park, Frenchay, Bristol, England.

When I went back upstairs, Nobomi was still sitting
looking out over the city. She let me sit near her, not in
Hugh's chair, of course I pulled up another and left his one
where it was. We weren't talking, she didn't seem to need
to. I took Hugh's piece of paper out and looked at it. Yes, I
thought it said Barbara. That was the name my mother
had whispered to me before she died. "Say thank you for
her every Mass now, Eva, you must", we're Catholics you
see. But she didn't say why.

Hugh didn't come again.

But there's more to this story. A lot more. Probably's more
than I ever knew even.

After that day Nobomi slowly became less isolated. She still went every afternoon to sit and look out over the city at the time Hugh used to be there. She arranged the chairs as they were when they had sat together, moving any others away, and it was as if, for her, he was there. She said nothing but if anyone went near she made it clear that she would not have anyone else sitting in his chair. Apart from this she seemed to want to be around us, the staff that is, mostly not the other girls, and she wanted to do things and help. In the end she was helping with the cleaning, carrying plates to the dining room, making beds, even looking after other girls if they were sick.

The talking came slowly and I was never sure how much that was because not talking had been a shock response to something that had happened to her or how much 'twas because she didn't have the language. Like I said, we still didn't know where she came from, fact was we never knew, right to the day she disappeared. She was African, and I doubt there were many African families living in Austria then, with Austria never having had any African colonies, not like most European countries. She did speak a very little English, but we didn't hear anything else in another language. You would have thought that she would have come out with something in her native language at some time, wouldn't you? But she never did. Over the months, as she picked up words, the natural way, the way a very young child does who is learning to speak, she became a good speaker of English. Not even English sounding like an Austrian or a German, because we had a teacher for a while who was the wife of a British diplomat and she came in to take language classes for the older girls. 'Course I spoke to Nobomi in English, because I am English, but she was very bright because she said to me once, "Eva, you are English like the teacher, but you do not sound like her." "Well," I said, "where I come from, we don't speak like teachers and such." I don't think she understood.

It's fair to say that Nobomi gave us some extra headaches. There were the usual ones – we had between twenty and thirty girls and they had ages from 8 to 18 and the staff were all women. Apart from all the 'internal' things like tantrums and moods and female adolescence, we had the constant worry about safety. We were better off than most because we were part of an organisation, we were the 'Inner Mission' of the Vienna Evangelical Hospital. Yea, that's funny, isn't it, me being brought up a Catholic and such. We were accommodated in the Alsergrund annexe not far from the old city, but it meant you had to know where we were if you wanted to find us. But we still got 'visitors' and we did need our Frau Winkel as chief door-keeper. If you are known to be difficult to get into, then that's a bit of a deterrent.

You have to remember how temporary and unofficial a lot of the services were then, in those years after the war. You would talk about 'welfare' services now, but then, well, you should really have called it 'survival' services. It meant that a lot of shelters appeared and disappeared very quickly and there was very little regulation right up to the time of the Treaty really – that's when the Occupation finished. You felt vulnerable all the time.

Where was I? Oh yes, we had the diplomat's wife coming in to teach English, and Nobomi joined her classes and worked very hard at that. We had to keep on getting her more books. The girls also did arithmetic and reading, in German of course, and some sewing and household skills. We were trying to set them up so that they could get a job as a domestic or seamstress or even clerk, so as they didn't fall prey to whatever male low-life might try to pick 'em up. They had to leave when they were 18, you see. That was a difficulty with Nobomi. We knew nothing about her. We didn't even know how old she was and she didn't seem sure herself. And when we asked her things like how she came to be in Vienna and where was her family from, she just went silent. Like there were years that were just empty for her. It wasn't that she got upset or tearful or even sad or nothing, she just seemed to go somewhere else in her head, then you couldn't get her back.

You see our problem. How were we to know when she had to leave? If we were honest, we didn't *want* her to leave and I wondered if there could be a way we could have her on the staff, she had done so much helping around the place over the years. Yes, years. She was with us 3 years and a few months. I always worried about our girls leaving. They came mostly as children, 11 or 12, but then they left as young women. They develop in their minds and ideas, and of course their bodies. If I'm honest, that's what worries me most. We do our best to make them aware, tell them what to look out for, keeping safe, all that, but they're not children any longer and all they want is to be grown up and do what *women* do.

That's why I worried about Nobomi. She was black. Well, like I said, very dark brown. And there was a lot of prejudice around. Hang over from the nazis of course, but prejudice anyway. So her colour was sure to be an issue sometimes. I mean, she couldn't hide very easily, could she? But I didn't know whether I was more worried about that or about her, well, her beauty. Any man would take one look and say she was special. She didn't seem to be completely African. I'm not an expert in anthropology and such, but I thought there must be some other blood in her line from somewhere. Her colour was quite dark, but not black, yea. Her hair was like African – small curls and black. But her nose had a bit of a European shape and her lips were not as full as an African's usually are. I say "usually", but who am I to say? I suppose I'm just going from pictures. But then her body – her breasts were not big and her hips were definitely slim. So, yes, special. That was the word. And a different sort of presence as well. If you saw her without catching her attention, perhaps during that hour every day when she sat looking out over the city, she had a serenity about her what nothing and no-one seemed to disturb, like she was somewhere else. She made me think of a native person looking out over some vast endless plane. Eh, listen to me – as if I know anythin' about Africa.

But anyways, all was well for 3 years and Nobomi seemed settled, in her way. She was a great help to all of us and I think she was a calming influence all round just by the way she was. It was sometime in April 1953 when her routine changed. I remember because it was about a month after Stalin died. You might think it strange I remember it that way when we were in the American zone and all, but my sister lived in the Russian zone down towards Baden. Baden was notorious because it was where they, the Soviets I mean, had their Tribunal and tried the spies they caught. Her flat-mate had an Austrian friend who was a domestic and was the 'girl-friend' of a Russian officer, only she had been bought by the Americans to get secrets. That's what happened, all sides tried to get domestics for spies, well-paid for the girls, but her Russian officer must have let out somethin' very sensitive, because it got back to his superiors some'ow and he was sent back to Moscow. Then they came for her. The Tribunal sentenced her to death – it was automatic for spying then – and sent her to Moscow as well. She must be dead, but no-one's ever told her family. She was unlucky because after Stalin died they stopped executing them, the Austrian girls who spied for the Americans.

So, sometime in April Nobomi's routine changed. She started going out, every day, after our meal at midday. Up to that time she had only gone out when we asked her to get some food or household things, but now it was every day. We were talking by that time, she and I, so once I asked her where she went and she said she went out to feel the 'big air'. Well, that fitted and we didn't have to keep them in when they got to her age – by now we assumed she was about 17 – so long as they were back by door-closing time. She always was, of course, much sooner in fact, she was usually out for about 3 hours or a little more in the afternoon.

I said she was special. And she was special to me. Perhaps that was because I was the one who admitted her. Or perhaps it was because I can't have no children and I felt I was looking after her. But one day I had to go out in the afternoon and I arranged that I went out just after her. And I followed her. I felt guilty straightaway of course, but I also so badly didn't want anything bad to be happening to her.

She walked like she knew where she was going, not dreamily at all. I was pleased she took the main street because I could follow her more easily without riskin' losing her or bein' seen. She was heading for the old city and she walked all the way down Währinger Strasse and at the end she didn't take the Ring, she crossed over and followed a straight line more or less until she came into Stephansplatz. She paused when she came to the cathedral's great door and looked like she was surveying the square. After a few moments she seemed to recognise where to go and walked across to one of the benches which were set at intervals along one side of the building. There was a man seated at this bench, he looked like a vagrant in a dirty heavy coat, very thin and haggard, almost hanging on the bench, and I wanted to shout out "No, No, No", but she went straight to the bench and sat down alongside him. I didn't see them speak, but I didn't stay too long. Of course I wanted to, I wanted to go up to 'er like she was my own daughter and take her away, but she wasn't mine, was she? Do you think I did right?

I was so relieved when she arrived back in the normal way that afternoon. I was fairly sure she hadn't seen me, but I felt very guilty anyways and I thought I ought to confess, so later on I went to her and told her what I had done and that I was worried she might be in danger from this down-and-out, because he might not have been what he seemed. The thing was, she didn't seem surprised, and she wasn't angry or nothin', she just looked at me calmly and smiled.

Then she said, "It was Hugh. We are going on a long journey to my ancestors' land when he is better." Well, I cried, of course. And she said, "I'll be ok, Eva. We'll both be ok." I was flabbergasted. That was the smart English officer? I could hardly believe…

Well, a few days later she went out as usual, but that time she didn't come back. We never saw her again.

I waited a few weeks, then I wrote to the person at the address Hugh had given me. Barbara. Funny really, coincidences – me coming from Bristol and all. Don't know why, it felt like joining up a circle.

hope receding...

Kurt

They brought him in at 4 in the morning. We had only been given an hour's notice and no instructions for holding. There was one cell left in the reception block so he went in there after we had stripped him and searched his clothes. They were allowed their clothes back after that if it was officially only "enquiry and investigation". Not arrested, they were told, we just need some information. (Arrest would have needed a four-power detention patrol.) The directive had come from high up – Aleksey Petrov, who had been the real second to Abakumov, when he had been Kommandant, and he seemed to be in the same position with the new chief, Arkady Boreyko. Never had a British officer brought in before though, if that's what he really was. Got some of our boys a bit unsettled.

Didn't dare show it of course, but you could tell. The hard ones leered and gloated, but mostly even they held off the pushes and trips and knee treatment. Not like with the Austrians – they were easy prey, especially the women, no status, mostly domestics or our officer's tarts, and once they got in here, no-one was ever going to see them again. Better if they had done away with themselves before we came for them. But a British officer. You'd have thought he would have been held at the Police HQ or the Military Tribunal in Baden, interrogated of course, but held for exchange. If they've put him with us, someone must know he won't be claimed.

We had been ordered to make no contact with the detainee, who had given his name as: 4574055 Lieutenant Winters. He had hammered on his cell door and shouted out quite frequently. We ignored it for long periods, but occasionally I sent someone to open the door grill, let him have his say, then shut the grill without making any reply. He gradually became more frantic; he swung between rage and pleading, but we followed orders and just let him say his piece, then closed the grill. He said he was within a few hours of being collected to be taken back to England, he was going home and he had left the army. Was he thinking that would make us sympathetic? There were plenty of men here who were wanting to go home. No mate, that's not the way to get round us. You got collected like you said you would, just not by your own side. They weren't smart enough. Got up too late.

Aleksey Petrov arrived in the afternoon. I stayed past my duty to be there when he arrived. I'd not met him before and he had been so tied in with Abakumov until he was called back to Moscow. That was enough reason to wait for him. He came alone and was not in uniform, which surprised me. It also surprised me that he wanted me to be in the interrogation with him, though with strict instructions to say absolutely nothing. But first he had the detainee put in the interrogation room and left on his own. Normal procedure to unsettle prisoners, but Petrov did everything to extremes. For instance, he hardly spoke and when he did it seemed only to provoke the other person. This time, after Winters had been installed as he ordered, he sat in my room and read some papers from his attaché case for a full hour without saying a word. Then he rose, put away his papers and motioned me to go before him into the interrogation room.

"We have met before, **Lieutenant** Winters. Not Mr Winters, it seems, as you told us then. But perhaps it is not even Winters."

"If you say so."

"I do and I would expect that with your training you would remember. We were introduced by Herr Koplenig, who believed that you were a reporter for The Times in London and that you could be trusted to help his Party and Soviet interests in Austria. I did not. But no matter, we have dealt with Herr Keller who had influenced Herr

Koplenig in that respect. You will have heard, I am sure. He fell in the Danube. The bullet in his head might have helped."

Winters did not reply. Petrov's gaze was expressionless.

"You have betrayed our trust, Lieutenant Winters. It is unlikely that Kommandant Boreyko will let you live. Unless I can attest to your usefulness to us. But that will not be easy. We are aware that you know nothing that is useful to us militarily. So what could you have that will save your skin? I will let you think about this, remembering that we have all the contents of your rooms, including all the letters. Until our next meeting, Lieutenant Winters."

That was all. After that Petrov left. His instructions were to continue the regime, ensuring no-one exchanged words with Winters, but occasionally (and irregularly) opening the grill, listening and noting what he said, but never replying. A week passed before he returned. During that time Winters made repeated demands to see the British consul saying that he had the rights of a British citizen because his commission in the army finished the day before our lads removed him. None of that made any difference now he was in our sector. Had he not heard of the American we caught a bit ago? The Yanks *wanted* us to charge him. He's in a gulag now. He won't ever come out. This Winters might be a bit different, though. You'd call him a spy, I suppose, but there seems to be something else. This business of our side at the top having trusted him.

What did he do, I wonder? Who got blamed? Who else's life is on the line, besides that Keller fellow, whoever he was? Is Petrov playing clever, or is he worried? Whichever it was, next time he played it differently. No waiting to unnerve him this time, he had us go straight in to get him off-guard.

"Salute when I enter."

"I have no commission. I am now a civilian. I cannot be required to salute."

"Very well, no protocol, then you will remain standing."

(From then on he was always made to stand during the interrogations.)

Now the silence. About 10 minutes, I should think, while Petrov read some papers he had brought in. Finally he spoke without looking up.

"Have you thought of what you have that might be enough to save your skin?"

"I am a British citizen and am entitled to see the British consul."

"Kommandant Boreyko does not think you are entitled to anything, not even your life. If you want him to change his mind, you will have to discover something you have which might do that."

"I will not collude with Soviet aggression."

"Very well. Remove him."

Then:

"Lieutenant Winters. Who is Harry?"

"I don't know any Harry."

"You are sure?"

"Yes."

"The Kommandant is interested in Harry. Think about it. If he gives you time."

That was all. Winters was returned to his cell. Petrov confirmed the same regime and then left immediately. For the next month or more this was all that happened, roughly once per week. Sometimes I got notice of Petrov's visits, sometimes not.

During that time Winters' manner and appearance in the interrogation started to change. His face was thinner and paler. His posture – he was always made to stand throughout – became less military and rigid and I thought I might have seen him sway very slightly on occasions, though Petrov, who rarely looked up from his papers on the desk, never seemed to catch this. His answers were identical, though, and his delivery unchanged.

I wondered when Petrov would become irritated and decide to increase the pressure. I also wondered what his objective was. He was not following our normal procedure of getting information and forcing a confession and then the detainee signing a protocol to present to the Military Tribunal for sentencing. And anyway, Petrov was too important to be acting as interrogator. Did Boreyko not know about Winters, I wondered? Was that just a tactic? It was obvious that Petrov and Winters had met. So was it all to do with Petrov?

I've seen different approaches taken by interrogators towards detainees depending on the sort of person they think they are – if they think he is a fearful person, then the interrogator will intimidate, maybe even take out his pistol and cock it and place it between them; if he thinks he is proud and touchy then he might be insulting; if the detainee seems to think himself important then the interrogator might be familiar with him. Anything to get him off balance, the opposite of what he is comfortable with. But usually it starts off seeming harmless, like they were really on the same side and just needing to understand things, like the detainee might have forgotten something or slipped up without noticing. But you could tell it wasn't quite like that with Winters. At this stage his military discipline didn't falter. And Petrov was feeding him what he was after – this Harry. But that was it. Apart from that, silence. Anything that would unnerve him.

After the first few months he must have decided it was time to increase the pressure. The regime was to suddenly change. We were to allow minimal sleep. A stronger light in the cell was to be kept on 24 hours. He had to sleep on his front with his arms hanging down the sides of the board. The grill was to be opened every 15 minutes and he was to be woken if he was asleep. During the day he had to be standing in the middle of the cell for 2 hours in the morning and 2 hours in the afternoon. You can be sure this new regime soon started to take a toll. He lost his military bearing. His eyes became distant and his face lost all expression. When he was taken along the corridor to the interrogation room he did little more than shuffle, so that the escort pushed him and punched him in the small of his back. In the interrogations Petrov did not alter what he said, but he made the silences longer. He also brought in a guard to stand behind him and jab him with his cane whenever his shoulders drooped or he started to sway. This regime continued for another few months and then we were told to increase the pressure again. We were to take away all his clothes and remove the bed from his cell. The bed had been a board supported on four blocks, but now the cell was completely bare except for his slop bucket and he had to lie face down on the stone flag floor to sleep. Of course sleep interruption was still in place.

Now I really started to think that all this with Winters was not really an interrogation at all. It was starting to seem very personal. I know this is difficult to understand if you are not in the Party, but interrogation isn't about the individual, it's about the Party. The individual has betrayed the Party, but he doesn't know that or he doesn't know how, so interrogation is to help him to tell us everything about his life so that we can show him how he has betrayed the Party and his countrymen. Then he can write his confession and the Tribunal can sentence him. With spies it's the same really, they might not be members of the Party, but communism is the right way for all people so they have betrayed their own kind, their own species if you like, and we are the ones who have to make sure that we keep things going safely and in the right direction for the good of mankind. The detainee, he is just the way we make this happen. He doesn't matter himself. It's not personal. But with Winters, it felt like it *was* him that mattered. It *was* personal. Sometimes it felt like Petrov was out for revenge on Winters, like Winters had caused him some actual harm.

For his next visit he told me to put Winters in the interrogation room before he arrived, he was to be naked – well of course he had never worn anything at all for months now – and standing, with a guard behind him to make sure he stayed rigidly upright and did not speak. I was to arrange the lights on either side of the desk so that they were shining straight in his face and he was to stand there for 3 hours before he himself arrived. He was not to be given any food that morning. When we went in I was to stand close beside Winters and on a signal from Petrov I was to shout very close to his ear, "Who is Harry?", alternately with Petrov.

I hadn't seen Winters for more than two weeks when I walked into that room. My step faltered, even seeing him from behind. He suddenly seemed a lot smaller, shoulders drooping, back curved over, hair thin and matted, no colour apart from a vivid red circle spreading on his back from where the guard was repeatedly prodding him with his stick whenever he moved, but it was his legs which alarmed me most. With standing for long periods the body fluids drain down into the legs, but his were so grossly swollen, even up into his thighs. It gets so that, standing or lying, the pain is excruciating. He should have had the doctor in. MVD[1] procedures are not that people die from torture. It is in the protocol that a doctor must examine at a certain point. But Petrov had instructed me not to admit the doctor. And I had complied. That is, I had avoided observing the prisoner.

Petrov had sat down behind the desk. He adjusted the lights. I was standing facing the prisoner's left-hand side, my head on a level with his. Petrov began gently as always.

"Lieutenant Winters, we need you to answer only one question and then all this will be over, we will be able to call the doctor and he will accompany you to our hospital wing where you will be given a bed until your health is returned, and when we are sure that you are strong enough to leave us and look after yourself in the city we will take you to a place of your choosing and ensure that you are safe. I think there is no more generous assurance I can give you.

"You know the question we need you to answer, but I will repeat it since you do not seem to be in good health today…

---

[1] The initials of the main Soviet security agency until 1954, when it was changed to KGB. It is now FSB.

"Who is Harry?"

Then a silence, but not for very long.

"Lieutenant Winters, I have told you this before, but I think it is fair that I tell you again now. We have everything that was in your rooms and we have examined everything and we have read all your letters. Surely you remember that Harry appears in your letters. The letters from someone called Barbara."

I thought I saw a twitch in his face when he heard "Barbara".

"So, Lieutenant Winters, who is Harry?"

That was the end of the gentle talking. After a few brief moments Petrov looked up sharply – his face, framed by the glaring lights, looked like the muzzle flame of a pistol shot – and he bellowed: "WHO IS HARRY?"

Then the double-barrel assault, Petrov in front and me yelling into his ear:

Who is Harry?

Who is Harry?

Who is Harry?

Who is Harry?

Who is Harry?

We went on until his legs gave way and he crumpled into a pitiful heap on the floor, the only indication of a human life being his wailing which grew and grew in intensity to a scream.

After a few minutes Petrov slowly rose from his chair and walked to the door, turning slightly when he reached it to indicate that I was to follow him. In the office he said that I was to add to Winters' regime an interrogation of this kind every second day. I was to use a senior guard to stand by him as I had and I was to take on his own role behind the desk. Each time we were to continue until he collapsed. He would not now be able to visit so often himself, but he would keep in contact to assess progress. I asked him how I would reach him to report if Winters gave us information about Harry. I did not expect the answer he gave: "He will not. Even if he does make something up, we are not interested in any Harry. You have no need to contact me."

Then he left and he never came back.

Of course, I didn't know Petrov was not coming back, so I followed his instructions and did his 'interrogations' every second day. But I did it without all the waiting and the soft talking, and after the first time, I didn't push it until he collapsed. His condition was getting worse all the time. Big blisters were forming on his legs. I called the doctor, but I told him he could not be transferred to the hospital. The doctor argued with me, but I thought I was still acting under Petrov's orders and I could not risk him arriving unannounced and finding Winters in the hospital.

The day after the doctor's inspection, they brought him to the interrogation room and before I started he said: "I want to speak." He was only just intelligible, his speaking very slow and slurred. When I gestured for him to do so, he said: "I can't give you what you want... only Harry... Barbara letter... died 50 years ago... if that is all... you want... I have nothing... just... kill me... now... please..."

I had Winters returned to his cell after that. I had to find a way to report this to Petrov. There was no point in continuing with this 'interrogation', no point in spending more time on this prisoner. And for me it raised a question of morality – Party morality of course – that it was one thing to put a prisoner through extreme humiliation and pain almost to the point of death if it served the Party code and contributed to the final victory of the Party for the People... I can do that... but if nothing can be won for the Party, then I cannot do it. At this point Winters should either be executed – his disappearance hidden of course – or he should be released.

I put a call through to the Dvortsa[2] where he was stationed with the Kommandant. But they could not

---

[2] Russian for Palace, which refers to the Palais Epstein, the HQ for the Soviet Kommandatura in Vienna. The nickname showed uncommon irony on the part of the Russian corps.

connect me. They denied there was an officer or operative of that name in HQ. It was not uncommon for a person's existence to be denied if they were engaged in sensitive operations, but I remembered the name of a warrant officer in Censors that I was once billeted with and I was able to be connected with him. He told me that Petrov had been reduced to general staff when Abakumov was called back to Moscow, because the new Kommandant had not wanted to inherit any suspicion through association with his predecessor's subordinates. More recently Petrov had himself been recalled to Moscow. (He said all this very quickly and quietly and immediately changed the subject, ignoring my surprise and further questions.)

Neither the MVD Handbook nor the Military Manual contains instructions for handling undocumented and unauthorised detention, which is what this now seemed to be. I believed the decision about what to do next was mine. I was the captain in charge of this Centre. Line responsibility for detainees was to the commander of the detaining authority. I had believed this to be Petrov, but now none existed and perhaps none had ever existed. This detention seemed to have been about revenge, and vengeance had been complete when Winters collapsed in the interrogation. From that moment he served no purpose for Petrov. The Party's protocols lead to execution or imprisonment, but both require sentencing, which can only be handed out to a documented detainee. Winters did not exist as a detainee. I had to either 'unofficially' execute him or find a way to release him.

At that point neither option was open to me. I could not release a man who could barely stand, and to execute him, well, I had no experience of that and could only think of taking him to the Danube where his body would be carried a sufficient distance before being discovered. Even so, to do this without help in his current condition would be impossible. I continued to 'interrogate' him every 3 or 4 days, but I changed the procedure. Officially, he had started to tell his story and so it could be more effective if I was alone with him and the guard was stationed outside the room. As he progressively complied with what the Party required of him, it would be normal to allow him 'privileges'. Over a period of several months I had the bed returned to his cell, relieved him of the standing routines, extended the intervals between waking calls finally allowing him 4 hours without interruption at night, increased his time allowance for eating and provided ample water all day, allowed him to sit during interrogations, and finally gave him back some clothes. On my orders, he now had regular visits from the doctor, but I continued to countermand the doctor's attempts to have him removed to the hospital. I wanted his recovery, to the extent that he would recover, assured, but only slowly. I wanted his presence and the routines around him to become habitual, then my colleagues would stop thinking about him as an individual and so he would go unnoticed and his final disappearance would attract the minimal interest. But don't mistake this as me caring for the man. At this stage I had not decided whether I was going to execute him or release him, but both of these options would require some cooperation on his part since neither could happen in the detention centre itself. So I saw it as a strategy for getting myself out of a situation for which there was no protocol, and, as far as those guys over in the Dvortsa were concerned, did not even exist.

But I was not prepared for what happened over the following months, no, almost two years, I suppose. It's strange how things can be changing gradually around you, one little thing after another but you don't notice anything on its own, and this goes on and you just carry on in your normal way, same old life, but then something makes you stop, you've seen something, and you suddenly notice how things *have* changed. You see you're not the same. Everything looks the same but you feel different about it. You'll be thinking I'm going a bit crazy, battle-hardened soldier and all that, now a chief gaoler, how's he talking like this? Well, fact is, I don't know. It's got me worried, I know that, no, more than that, scared I think if I'm honest. If I hadn't seen this coming, what else didn't I see? And what might someone else have seen that I didn't?

In the beginning, when I realised something had happened, I still didn't know how or what was different that would have caused it. You see, I didn't put it together that what I was doing with Winters was changing *me*. I'm not a psychiatrist or anything, I'm no Freud, so I can't put things in a clever way, the best I can do is – we don't do anything on our own and we never come out the same as we went in, like something always crosses over, whether we notice or not. Take that day after my kid had been ill in the night and I had driven him to hospital and they didn't know what was the matter so they kept him there… and me and my wife, we didn't sleep at all that night… so Winters had sat down the next day – I was letting him sit during the interrogation by this time – and he started:

"We're late."

"How do you know we're late? You've got nothing to tell you the time."

"You're telling me." And then: "You've hurt me. Been cruel. Taken everything. Now, I *need* this."

Then after a pause and looking straight at me: "But we're late. Something happened."

I tell you I had to catch myself to not say sorry and tell him why.

A few weeks later the guard came to me and said he could not get him out of his cell. He was screaming in a corner, holding his arms out as if shielding himself from blows, then putting his hands over his ears and yelling "Not him, Not him." I had forbidden coercive force for Winters, so the guard wanted permission to manhandle him into the interrogation. I refused and went with the guard to his cell. Winters was still in a corner making an unreal animal-like noise between a groan and a scream. I stood facing him and said: "We're late." Then I remembered and I added, "Something happened." He slowly recovered and followed me out of the cell and down the corridor to the interrogation room.

It was probably then that I knew I wasn't going to put a bullet in his head and throw him in the Danube. Not that I admitted it of course even to myself, I needed to go on denying that anything had changed, that I had changed, but I knew really. It went on a long time, the routine we were now into, it had to because he was a long time getting back to some sort of health, longer than I expected, his legs, they were bad. But his speaking got better and he wanted to eat again, so gradually he looked less like a skeleton but still very gaunt and thin. I got to thinking there was a chance I could take him out into the city and point him towards a hostel and he would make it to the door before he fell over. Far enough at least for me to drive away. But I still couldn't see how the opportunity was going to come up.

In the end, events 2000 kilometres from Vienna in March 1953 gave me my chance. On 6th March in the early hours, the announcement of Stalin's death came on our radio, which relayed the Moscow Home Service. There had been rumours two days before because Pravda had said he was very ill, so the atmosphere had been a bit unreal. All ranks knew that a lot could change. People became reluctant to challenge what was happening in case it meant they were acting in conflict with new protocols.

The Military Tribunal in Baden even suspended its sessions from 4th March in case sentencing regulations changed. I saw my opportunity and in spite of spending most of the night listening to the radio, I arrived early at our barracks, commandeered a car without driver, telling the officer in charge that orders had come during the night from the Dvortsa to transfer Winters to them pending a demand from Moscow and the new order. It sounded official and it fitted with everything that was going on.

I am not proud of what I did. I admit that. But I was nervous. I needed to be back, return the car and be calmly at my station before it occurred to anyone that one of the detainees was no longer there. The duty guard knew, of course, I would have to arrange something with him, but no-one else should give it a passing thought.

It was early, still dark. I drove into the Old City and stopped on one side of Stephansplatz. I didn't want to be seen with him, so I hustled him out of the car and left him sitting on one of those seats along the side of the Cathedral. And then, I just walked away. No words, just walked away, left him. No, I'm not proud of doing it that way. But you can understand, can't you?

I've no idea what happened after that. I was decommissioned within the year. It had never seemed the same again. Like something had crossed over.

from the author's journal…

Are we ever un-involved? If something "crosses over" with every encounter, then it can never be just **my** life. So perhaps we have to say that a life is not something that can be owned, it can only be shared. Or do we have to go further still… BY DEFINITION it is shared. The tradition of Nobomi's people was <u>ubuntu</u>, which I had thought I understood… and then I heard another story… and another…

simply waiting...

Onlooker

Louie is confused by the two figures she sees across the other side of Stephansplatz sitting on one of the seats along the wall of the Cathedral. For a long time she is unable to work out where her puzzlement is coming from. The nearest she can get is that they didn't belong together, or rather, in *her* mind, they hadn't come together.

It was 4 years since she had been to the Salzburg festival and the last time she came she had also come via Vienna. Before then it had been almost 30 years, and that had been her first visit to the city – barely 3 years after the end of the First War. The conditions that first time had been heart-rending. She wondered now why she had come at all that year, the journey had been long and very tiring and the grandeur which she had been expecting to be overawed by, was tarnished and degraded. She remembered her heart had sunk on her first walk round the Old City. But she had met some 'lovely girls' (as she remembered them) who were running food centres for children and she had even become part of their team, for the time she was in the city.

That was 1921. Now it was 1953 and she was standing on the same spot, as far she could make out, looking across the expanse of old paving at the imposing bulk of the Dom… and wasn't this the same place as when she had been trying to get a photograph of the cathedral just 3 years before, and she'd been walking backwards without looking and almost fallen over this young girl who ran off across the square? No-one behind her to fall over today, hardly anyone at all around this early, just those two people sitting on the seat over there. "But what's this odd feeling I have that they don't belong together? How would I know? Oh I am such a silly." Still curious, she walks slowly across the square, then stops and takes up a sightseer stance, standing at an angle, casting her glance all round, even craning her neck to see the top of the spire, before casually moving her gaze past the two people on the seat, though in fact she need not have been so churlish about not attracting attention because neither showed any sign of even having noticed her.

Louie knows two things about herself, which she delights in giving free rein to whenever the opportunity arises: one is that her intuition about people, especially men, is reliable (this makes her chuckle, never having had a 'beau' herself); and the other is that she can make anybody like her because she 'is such a silly'.

She walks on over until she is standing quite close and in front of them.

"Hello. I have seen both of you before, but I am not sure where and you were not together.

"But I like it when people appear again out of the past."

They look at her, not with any discomfort or annoyance, just look, as one might gaze over the terraces of time and life – rapt, wistful.

"Thank you for not shooing me away." Louie makes to walk on, but the girl holds out her arm and motions for her to sit down beside her.

So now there are three people on the seat outside St. Stephen's cathedral in Vienna in the early morning of 1st June 1953. And if you had seen them, I think *you* might now be puzzled too. I will try to describe what you are seeing.

The seat is typical of town seats from the early part of the century throughout central European towns and cities, with overly ornate cast iron end-blocks holding solid wooden – oak perhaps – slats, which had been variously painted, over the years, but were now mainly bare and untreated. (Towards the end of the century they would be removed and replaced by concrete-framed affairs, still with wooden slats but varnished unconvincingly, and spaced around the square so that visitors could sit looking towards the cathedral instead of out from its walls.) You may be wondering why I spend so many words on the seat, and yet, seats so often colour our picture of their incumbents. As it is, the image of these three people, sitting as one is bound to sit on such a municipal bench, completely belies each of their natures and backgrounds.

On the left as you are looking at them, is Louie, who personifies that old-fashioned styling of 'English Gentlelady'. Spinster, of course (though not I believe from choice), she has an air of leftover Edwardian England about her. Sitting quite upright without a hat, carrying a zipped-up crocheted shoulder bag, and wearing a twenties frock which is a rather prim concession to summer leisurewear, her appearance, despite the formal pose, has a flow, but not in a surging way, more like the inner leaves of a willow tree fluttering in the breeze. Perhaps it is her roundish face, which holds the folds of successions of smiles, and the way her movements constantly imply a gentle uncomplicated interest in those close by, head inclined, always turning attentively towards a companion; perhaps it is her voice, high and slightly squeaky, which seems to tinkle like a mountain stream.

In the middle is an African girl of around 18 sitting with a stillness which seems to be in her mind and not just her body, but a stillness that is without uneasiness, more like patient waiting, in the way that seems so natural to people of that continent. She is slim, her hair is black and curly, and her dark brown eyes seem to look out into a world which stretches way beyond the world *we* mostly see.

And then there is a man whose age you might roughly guess as mid-30s, though his dishevelled state really suggests at least another 10 years. Although the early morning is bright and sunny and warm he is enveloped in what might once have been an army greatcoat but which would surely hang very loose now on his gaunt frame were he to stand up. His hair is straggly and his face, pale, with hollow cheeks and lined forehead, appears unshaven with an uneven stubble, though perhaps it is not always so. His look, his eyes, appear more uncomprehending than vacant. But he pulls himself up as Louie sits down.

Louie, who seems to assume without hesitation that the other two will speak English, turns to the girl and says, "I am a visitor here. I have been three times before and each time I am in Vienna I come to this square. I am thinking you must live here, but is this where your family are from, my dear?"

"My family lived in Gqeberha, but I don't know my people any more. Everything changed and a man brought me away from there and then I lived here. But now Hugh is going to take me back to the land of my ancestors. We are starting when he is well again." She glanced towards the man.

"It will be a long way, won't it?"

"I think so. It is in Africa. In the south."

"I wonder how you will get there."

"We don't know. But there will be a way. We must wait. I am Xhosa and my people were called Mfengu. They were known as wanderers because they had to move from their homelands with the wars and in the end they became part of the Xhosa, who let them in."

"I am interested in families and where they came from and how they moved around so that they ended up where they are. Don't we always feel we need to keep a connection?"

"We believe our ancestors can see the people we are and affect what happens sometimes."

"I think that too, in a funny way. I think we never completely lose what other people have given us, especially our families, and their families have given them, back and back."

"I don't remember my father. He was taken away by government men. After that, we were in a house with my grandmother. My mother was there as well, I think." She goes quiet. The man moves a little, he seems sensitive to her.

"You've had a troubled life, my dear. And so young."

"My grandmother taught me that life goes on and then we take our place with our ancestors and we become ancestors in our turn."

"You know, I think that is a very good way of seeing it…

"Can I tell you about my family in England when I was about your age? I think I am probably old enough to be your grandmother. I wonder what it would be like for me to meet *your* grandmother? Do you know whether she is still alive?"

"I don't know. Maybe she will still be there when we get to my homeland."

"Well, I had two sisters and three brothers and I was the youngest except one. The youngest was Harry and he went away following another brother, who was called Frank, to South Africa. I don't remember them talking about that place you said. They were in a place called East London, it was on the coast."

"I think East London is the place we call eMonti, it's not far from…"

Her words tail off as she feels the man becoming distressed beside her. His body had gone stiff as he forced himself against the back of the seat, his eyes wide open in a terrified stare. She turns to him quickly and takes his hand. "Hugh, Hugh, they're not here, it's me, it's Nobomi, I am staying Hugh, there is a lady here who is talking to us, but *they're* not here, Hugh, we are in the square where you first found me and it's a sunny day, we're outside Hugh, there are no walls, no walls here."

His breathing, which had become a frantic gasping, slowly begins to subside to a normal rate, his rigidly stiffened body gradually relaxes. Then the girl, still holding his hand, turns back to Louie, who can feel her own heart fluttering uncomfortably.

"Did you say you knew East London… eMonti?"

"Yes, my grandmother lived there and my mother was born there."

Now it is Louie's turn for distress, though not in the violent way of the man. She reaches for her handkerchief to dab her face in comfort and looks out over the square, feeling herself very flustered, thinking, – Oh dear, this cannot be right… dear me, surely… I really shouldn't be here… Then, after a pause, and quite sternly – Come on Louisa, don't be such a silly.

She takes a deep breath and turns back to the girl.

"You said your grandmother lived in East London?"

"Yes."

"And your mother was born there?"

"Yes."

Louie wondered whether she would dare to go on.

"Is your grandmother's name also Nobomi?"

"Yes."

"And your mother's name, was it, oh dear I can't pronounce it very well... Ngoxolo?"

"Yes." The girl is starting to look perplexed.

"This is the last question, my dear, and then I will tell you what is in my mind." She pauses, "The picture in the locket you are wearing... – the girl is surprised and looks down at her locket – "...is it a white lady holding a white cat?"

Now the girl looks alarmed, "But I have only shown it to Hugh."

"It is alright, my dear. I saw your locket a long long time before you showed it to Hugh. A long time before it was given to you. If you want, I will tell you how you come to have it. But I think we should have a little rest while you look after Hugh and when you think he is ready and might be able to listen as well, then you tell me. I will just wait until you say it is the time to start."

While Louie occupies herself watching the scattered movements around the square, the sporadic signs of life gathering pace again on a brightly hopeful summer morning, the girl and the man become absorbed each in the other, their conversation muted and personal, but not in a lovers' way, or even carer-patient, it seems more equal than that, as if each has their own stake in the other's wellbeing.

After a while, the girl turns back to Louie: "I think it is time now."

Louie takes a deep breath.

"Well, the story – your story – from when my family became a part of it, yes, we have a connection you and I – begins in 1901. That was the year my youngest brother, whose name was Harry (she glanced quickly at the man, but he seemed to be listening calmly) followed his brother, whose name was Frank, to South Africa. Up to then there were six of us living with our parents in a city in England called Bristol (now she noticed a flicker of recognition on the man's face). Well, Frank had gone to South Africa the year before and in 1901 Harry got a passage on a steamship and went to join him. They were young men after adventure – Frank was 20 and Harry was 17. At the same time as Harry was on his way to South Africa, your grandmother Nobomi, who I think was the same age as Harry, was walking from where her family lived in a little place called Matatiele – that is right up where the mountains come down to the planes – to eMonti, which Frank and Harry knew as East London. It took your grandmother almost two years to get from Matatiele to East London and when she arrived she wanted to send a telegram to her family to tell them that she was safe. That's how she met Harry, because Harry was the telegraph clerk in the Post Office, and he sent it for free because she didn't have much money and it would have been quite expensive. He left a note for her to tell her he had sent it and he put his address on the note in case she needed more help.

"Well, nothing happened for a while, but then in the middle of one night Harry heard a banging on his door, and it was your grandmother, Nobomi. Some men where she was living had done something very nasty – ohhh, I can't even think about it, oh dear, no, it was too awful – but she had escaped, and now she had nowhere to go and the only address she had was Harry's. Well, as you will guess, she stayed, and they fell in love and before very long your grandmother knew she was pregnant. Her baby was going to be your mother: Harry was your mother's father.

"Now things became very difficult, not because Harry did not love your grandmother, he loved her very very much, but because he could not work out what would be best for your grandmother and their child. You see, things were starting to get very unpleasant in South Africa where they were living, there were different native peoples and some sided with the English, others with the Dutch, and some wanted no white people, but mostly the white people didn't want African people to live in their towns and they wouldn't pay them properly – I think you know the sort of things that happened, Nobomi, because it got much worse. But I'm talking about Harry, aren't I? He could not work out what to do for the best. He used to go swimming when he wanted to clear his mind so that he could work things out, he was a good swimmer, but one evening he went out in the Ocean and he didn't come back. His body was washed ashore a few days later and he is buried in the cemetery in East London. We know which his grave is.

"That was your grandfather, Nobomi. I am sorry. He died before your mother was born. My other brother Frank wrote to us and told us all this and our mother wanted Harry's girl-friend (because they were never able to get married you see), the mother of his daughter, to have something from our family. That is the locket you are wearing. The lady in your locket is her mother, one of your great great grandmothers, one of your ancestors. I know all this because, as my mother told me to, I put the locket with a letter that I sent to Frank, so that he could give it to your grandmother.

"Our father went to South Africa to see your grandmother and he stayed a long time so that he could see your mother and hold her as a new-born baby, but he knew he could not take them back to England because they belonged in Africa. Your grandmother stayed with Frank a little while longer after our father had gone home, but life was becoming very difficult – all the regulations and segregation – Frank did his best and he kept her safe, but in the end she decided she must go. And so she left one morning while he was at work. He stayed on for many months in case she came back, but there was no sign of her. We never knew where she went. We were very sad and we just hoped that she would find people who would help her and look after her. We just hoped. And now, here *you* are, another Nobomi. So somewhere in between, something was right. It makes me so happy to know you are here."

Louie reaches for her handkerchief again. "Oh dear, I'm happy and I'm crying. What a silly."

They are quiet, all three, until the girl turns to Louie: "I knew something was different for me. Thank you for finding me."

Then the man, who is looking out across the square, seeming to spy something from a great distance, says: "I gave someone a white cat once, I can't remember where, it was a long time ago." And Louie suddenly realises how it had been that the images of these two people on the bench could have come to her as people she had met, but could not put together. It had been on a train from Vienna to Salzburg. That man who said he was a soldier, but wasn't in uniform, he had been a good talker – she remembered she had both warmed to him for that (she was a chatterbox herself) and been wary of him at the same time. He had seemed to be wanting advice on his love life – from her of all people! – mentioned a girl, and this porcelain cat he might buy for her… "I don't think he told me her name"… "but I don't think it was this girl, these two are not lovers and this girl would have been very young then, no, it's something else with them"… and she let herself dream a little… "oh the world is such a wonderfully strange and frightening place"… but where did 'frightening' come from just then? true of course, but why at that moment? Something to do with the man. Could the man on the train and the man sitting on this seat *really* be the same man? He had been smart on the train, and now… But she is sure that he must be. And now her intuition is nagging her again though differently and it is something to do with a girl, but not this girl, another girl… "this is all becoming a bit of a muddle, oh dear."

The man speaks again, softly: "Bristol", but that is all he says. Now he seems to be falling asleep. But Louie has caught the word and jumps slightly – no, not possible, can't be, too much coincidence – and dismisses her "silly thought".

To the girl, as the man sleeps: "When do you think you will start your journey?"

"I remember my mother told me that things will happen when their time comes and it is for us to find our place along the way."

"Your mother was wise. I am sorry you do not still have her to help you."

"My mother was for everybody. Perhaps that was because Harry was her father."

"I remember Harry looked at life quite like that. He believed we take what comes and accept it, even if that means we have to change our plans and ideas. And I think he believed that, in the end, all will be well. That seems very optimistic, doesn't it? But I am sure he thought that if we don't struggle against life too hard, we can enjoy what it gives us much more."

The girl bows her head. "My mother struggled. They killed her. I was very young. I couldn't help her."

The man stirs and the girl turns to him to help him get more comfortable. Louie remembers she must soon catch her train to Salzburg and then wonders if she might forget the festival altogether this year and stay here in Vienna instead and maybe if she did that she could see Nobomi again and hear more about her story and her mother's story... then she hears a quiet voice inside her saying, "don't follow, Lou, it isn't a rose-garden… things must happen when their time comes." And so she turns to Nobomi: "If I give you my address, will you write to me one day and tell me how things have worked out for you, your journey, finding your grandmother?"

"I will, but I might not find my grandmother, she might be dead."

"I will wish with all my heart that Nobomi will find Nobomi. That has a lovely ring to it, doesn't it."

Louie recovers a pen and some paper from the muddle of her bag, writes her name and address and gives it to the girl. Then she gets up, and noticing that the man is still sleeping, says, "Goodbye Nobomi, I am so happy we have met."

The girl smiles broadly: "Ntlela-ntle. Enkosi kakhulu."[3]

Louie gets up, smiles, then turns and walks away. She doesn't look back. She never does.

---

[3] "Goodbye. Thank you."

being alone...

Nobomi

My name is Nobomi. In your language it means Life.

I am scared. I have no home. I am a mother. My daughter's only home is me. Her name is Ngoxolo. It means Peace. But we have no peace.

This is my land, but I do not know my place in it.

I do not know where to look for my people.

Somewhere is my family, but I do not know the way back to them, and I think they would not know me.

Somewhere in this land my ancestors are buried, but I think they will be sad. Or maybe they are angry.

Last night I had a dream.

In my dream I was running over sand and behind me was
the Ocean and in front I could see the hills of my
homeland, but they were not coming any closer even as I
was running with all my strength. Then I was in a kraal
and I thought I was alone, but something moved through
the trees on one side and it was a mbulu. It was very dark
and I was very afraid because I knew it was a mbulu.
Their hands are like claws, but they can take on the shape
of people and hide their tails. This one was like a man, but
I saw its tail so I knew it was a mbulu. Then something
moved on the other side of me and it was another mbulu,
but that one was quite light coloured and it was carrying
something in a pouch, holding it like a baby and I could
see it was Ngoxolo, so I ran to take her from it but the
dark mbulu was faster than me and it snatched Ngoxolo
from the arms of the light mbulu and ran out of the kraal.
Now we were running into the hills, but the dark and the
light mbulu got to the hills before me and started fighting
and then more dark ones came and were fighting the light
one. Then I was on the shore of the Ocean again and I
looked down at my feet and I could see Ngoxolo lying on
the sand, but she seemed such a long long way off and
very small and she didn't move or make a sound. A big
wave came and nearly knocked me over and when it drew
back into the Ocean there was nothing on the sand.
Ngoxolo had gone.

I do not remember how I knew I was awake now. I lay completely still. I did not dare to move in case she wasn't there beside me. My mind and my body were fighting, locked together, they held each other with iron claws, I could not move, I felt nothing except... terror...

When Frank told me Harry had been found washed up on the beach I had screamed and I beat his chest with my fists because he had made my Harry dead... but really I already knew, deep inside I knew...

Last night I had to stay completely still. I could not bear to know again. She was Harry living. Ngoxolo. She must not go as well.

East London Dispatch…

Adam

"I was young back then, a 'rookie' as the English say, a photo-journalist on the local paper, just out of school. I'd always been interested in photographing things, especially with the new cameras not being so difficult to carry around and you didn't have to do everything in a studio or spend ages setting up outside with a tripod and then having to re-site it all every time you wanted to change an angle. I was really excited when the Dispatch bought one of the new Monocular Duplex cameras. It was called an artist's camera because you held it waist-height and looked down and saw the image the right way up and exactly as it was going to appear, because you were looking through the camera's lens. Better still you could walk around and find the angle you wanted easily. So that sold it for me,when the Dispatch said I could use their latest and best. I should mention they had even bought the expensive version which took the new roll-film, so no more clumsy plates.

"I suppose, if I'm honest, I was a little nervous, for a bit. anyway. Well, you see, being Austrian and that. There were a few of us in the town, Austrians, Germans, a little community really, we had our own few streets, but the town was really English. It was a small Xhosa village at the mouth of the river originally – the Xhosa called it eMonti – but they were on the edge of town now, because the army had advanced to establish the border of Eastern Cape after the latest native wars last century. Now there was a garrison on the Cape side of the river, but most of the residential and commercial parts were on the east side, the Transkei it was called, the land the British pretended was still for the native tribes to govern. But here was this town of mostly English people, trying to be a 'home from home' I think you say. They even called the main shopping street Oxford Street. So that was why I was a bit nervous – the Council and the people in control were English and so the newspaper had to keep in step. Even though the British and German governments were co-operating on a few things when it suited them, there was always tension underneath. But you understand, we didn't know then what was going to happen 10 years or so later.

"I think I was also nervous because I had had this idea that you could do reporting and journalism differently with these new cameras. It didn't take five minutes and more to get a picture, it took about 30 seconds. You didn't have to arrange your subjects, then go back to the camera and check everyone was in the shot, then wave your arms around to get people to move this way or that, then tell people it was coming and they had to stay completely still and keep looking however they were supposed to look, until you told them it was over. I thought, wouldn't it be great if photographs could be natural, like you were taking a slice of life and showing it to people? And now you could.

"Like I said, I was just a rookie, and this must have sounded like a revolution to those loyal retainers, who wanted the Dispatch to be a Times or a Standard or one of those temples of journalism in London. But this was *East* London on the far tip of another continent almost 10,000 miles from London. So I had a fight on my hands. But I always thought Mr. Crosby had the same ideas really. He was the editor-in-chief, well thought of and an innovator, but even he had to win over the directors. He managed, though. Slowly. And I kept on submitting pictures and stories which were closer and closer to how things really looked as they were happening. He only used the odd one at first, but little by little he put more in until, after I had been there about four months, he put one of mine on the front page. That caused a real stir because our layout wasn't designed like that, to have a picture story on the front.

"The story that was really happening, which was running along below the surface, affecting everything, but only gradually, so that people were taken up with each incident that happened day to day and not really seeing the trend, well, that was segregation. 'That's where you come in, Adam,' Mr Crosby said to me, 'I want people to know what's happening from the bottom up: take your pictures and write your stories so that when our readers read them, they will *feel* what it's like.'

"I met Frank not long after I joined the Dispatch. He was an engineer and he wanted me to do some technical photographs of a winch for a catalogue. I was not going to do freelance now I had a full-time job, but a friend introduced us so I agreed. We got on well, perhaps it was him being an engineer and us Germans liking things to be precise and well-made. We were both about the same age and I thought we might become friends, spend some evenings together, but after work was over he always left very quickly and I never found out anything about him. Until he asked me if I would do a portrait for him in his house. I thought he meant a portrait of himself for his portfolio or something, but he said no, another person, but I had to promise I would not tell anyone and I had to make sure that I did not leave any trace of it at the Dispatch – because of course I would have to use their equipment. When I agreed he told me the portrait would be a girl and a baby. I remember how he told me. He paused after saying that, and then went on – 'a Xhosa girl'

– and he paused again, and then – 'my brother's girl-friend… but my brother is dead.'

"He went very quiet after that. He just told me where he lived and we agreed a time. He seemed to go into himself. We had been chatting up till that point, just being sociable, but now he became the engineer again, putting things in place on his desk, putting papers in folders, then he left – very courteous, the reserved English professional.

"A couple of days later I went to his house in the evening as arranged. I took the new camera I was telling you about. I wouldn't normally have used that one for a formal portrait, which is what Frank seemed to want, but I didn't want to attract people's attention by taking equipment out that would normally stay in the offices, plate camera, tripod, hood, it might have made a commotion. So I took the new Artist's Camera.

"When I got there the girl, Nobomi was her name, was nervous. I could tell she was not from round here, even though there are a lot of Xhosa around East London. I thought she might be from the far country. She had a serenity about her, even though she was nervous. Her eyes were dark brown, so dark it was like you were looking into the depths of the earth. Her baby was very young, only a few weeks I think, and it had the first wisps of curly hair. I took several exposures so that I could select the best. When it was over she said to me, "Thank you, Mr Neumann. This is my daughter Ngoxolo. We wanted her grandmother to be able to see her. You have made that possible." Then she and the baby went into another room and Frank drank a beer with me outside on the platform. That was it really. Just another private job. I gave Frank the two photograph copies he wanted when I next called at his office. It was 23 years before I saw Nobomi and her daughter again, but that's a story for another time.

"The next time I saw Frank was three weeks later when I happened to be passing his house and he was sitting out on his platform with a beer. He had an oil lamp burning or I might not have seen him, but he called me up for a drink. He seemed to be pleased for the company. The girl had left with her daughter. He was worried about her. He was keeping the lamp burning every night so that she knew she could come back. He had no idea where she had gone, but he thought she might be trying to get back to her family and that worried him because they were almost 200 miles away, in the foothills of the Drakensberg mountains. I said he must feel very lonely without her. He said he felt lost and unsettled. When I said that it was always difficult when we lose the girl we love, he told me quickly I had got it wrong. 'She was my brother Harry's girlfriend and Ngoxolo is his daughter. After Harry died I looked after them. At first it was out of loyalty – you can't turn out a mother and a baby, can you? – but then things changed. Nobomi became very depressed and I helped her look after the baby and we became like a family – not a family like being married, we had separate rooms, we never, you know. But it became part of me, to be looking after them and if she wasn't well, I didn't feel right either. No, it wasn't romantic. But it was a kind of love, I suppose. Father would have called it the man's duty, but that's not right either. Nobomi had a word for it. She said it was *ubuntu,* what we had.' He went quiet for a while, then, 'We only hugged once, you know, that was the evening before she left. I suppose I should have known then. The next day I kept looking at the clock in the office – that's not like me – and I rushed back home, but I was too late. Much too late I think.'

"We sat without speaking for several minutes. Then he said, 'If I just knew they were alright, safe, that would be enough, because she would be doing what she believed in. Yes, that would be enough for me. I don't need her to be here with me. I think that's what she meant by *ubuntu.'*

"I thought to myself – Come on, Adam, you work for a newspaper, you have a better chance of finding her than most people. And Mr Crosby, he doesn't go with all this segregation, even though he's English. Down in Port Elizabeth they call people like him liberals. – So I told Frank I would try to find out about her, just so that he could know they were safe, if that was enough.

"And that was how we parted that evening. But I never did find any trace of Nobomi. Mr Crosby tried as well. No, she had vanished. But I did run into Frank again."

~~~

Again... no, not again, they're pushing me down... it's so cold, so cold... light, the blinding light... the water...

Don't breathe in, not yet... I need air... no, don't breathe... air...

Harry, Lieutenant Winters, we want to know about Harry

I don't know Harry

We think you do. You must remember better. Then nothing more need happen to you

No Harry... no Harry... don't know...

Again then

No... no... no...

Hugh, look at me, look at me, they're not here any more... just me, Nobomi

Did they find Harry?

There is no Harry

I don't know Harry... I can't tell them

There's only us here, Hugh, there's no-one to hurt you

Will I find her?

I don't know, Hugh, I don't know

~~~

"I hadn't seen Frank for almost a year when he turned up downstairs in the reception asking for me. Our girl at the front desk had come across to the bottom of the stairs and yelled up for me, as she usually did – lucky Mr Crosby wasn't around, he didn't like her shouting – so I came down and there was Frank looking a bit agitated waving a copy of the Dispatch which he had open at an inside page. He put it down on the desk, oblivious to the disapproval of the girl who had to shift her work across to the end, and pointed at one of the pictures of an incident that had occurred a few weekends before up at Mdantsane. As it happened I had covered the story as reporter and photographer – it was one of Mr Crosby's 'show it as it is, Adam' missions. So that's what I had done. There had been a confrontation between a few employers from East London who had gone up to Mdantsane because some workers had stopped turning up for work at the same time as tools and some money had gone missing. So they had gone up with their foremen and factory guards and smashed up a few houses looking for what they thought the workmen had taken. I had managed to get a few shots through open doorways of the rampage through people's homes, but the worst trouble happened when the employers' gangs were on their way back and they were blocked by local young native lads who had clubs. They were brave, God they were brave – excuse my blasphemy – because the employers' gangs had iron bars and I saw a few with rifles too. The fighting had lasted almost an hour and I was trying to get the angles that would make the readers think – all this over a few tools and a bit of cash for some of the poorest people for miles around? – I had to take cover myself several times. But the picture Frank was pointing to was one where a mother was trying to pull her boy, who was on the ground injured, out of the way of the brawl around him. She was on the ground herself and you could see her straining with desperation in her eyes as she struggled to get him clear.

"But it wasn't that woman that Frank was looking at, no, he was wanting me to look at another woman on the edge of the crowd, who was sideways to the camera and clutching a child to her and looking like she was trying to get clear. 'That's her,' he said, 'that's Nobomi, I'm sure it is. Can you remember taking this shot, can you remember, Adam, was she alright?'

"But of course, I couldn't remember. If you had been there you would understand. At one point the battle engulfed me and I was lucky to get out. That might have been when I took this one. I looked closely. You really could not see clearly because of all the bodies casting shadows, but I took Frank upstairs and got out my magnifier and we both looked again. In the end we agreed that it probably was not Nobomi. I felt sad for him. The way he was that afternoon, the way he seemed to be willing it to be her, it was the closest I saw him to being the distraught lover: he seemed to want her back with him so much, and I believe a bit of that was for him too, not just for her.

"It brought us together again, though, and I went round to his house that evening for some beers. We sat on his platform well into the night.

"He asked me if I had a brother and I told him I had no brother or sister. I waited while he seemed to be weighing something up in his mind. Then he began, 'Harry only came out here because of me. I had been here about a year, just to see a bit of the world before I settled down in a profession, and I knew they were looking for engineers here and it might turn into something. I wrote to him and suggested he try it as well because new things, different things, always intrigued him. I said I would find him a job, so he came. I found him a clerk's job in the post office. He did alright, progressed a bit. That's how he met Nobomi. She had come in to send a telegraph message back to her family and Harry was on duty. She was a girl from way up-country just arrived in town. A few days later she turned up at his lodgings in the middle of the night. She had been raped by some of her own and Harry's was the only address she had. That's how they started. He took her in, I remember he didn't make anything special of it, she was just there. I don't think they were lovers for a while. He was like that, he just let things happen and lived with whatever came. I envied him for that, because I have always been someone who needed to work things out and have a plan and know what I would do next. Know the way forward, look after things. Not Harry. He accepted things as they came. People too.'

"A silence took over. Frank had stopped. It felt like the world had stopped. I saw us like a painting – two men sitting at a table in the almost dark, the only light the oil lamp flickering yellow on our faces and even our beer mugs unheeded for that while... 'He drowned. And I was angry, so angry with him. He would change our lives for ever and he had not let me in. He left the mother of his unborn child. He left his own mother, and he was her favourite. He left me. And I would have found a way. Somehow I would have found a way' – Did Frank mean that it was intentional? – 'He let me down, I wanted to be more like him, I was trying, I thought it was the way to feel at ease, be content, but now it seemed when life was at its hardest, Harry's way didn't work. So perhaps we are safer if we keep ourselves well buttoned-up?'

"I had no answer. I was sure he did not want an answer.

"After we had re-filled our mugs, we talked more generally, but it could not be said that the pervading tone of our conversation lightened very much. We talked about the creeping segregation, and yes, we wondered about Ngoxolo, Harry and Nobomi's daughter, and where she would fit in when she grew up, her roots from different soils. We lamented the waste from conflicts, which Frank himself had felt in such a personal physical way through the loss of his leg. We wondered what it is in Man that he is so prone to destroy, when the prizes of collaboration are so much greater. Yes, that's right, bear-mug philosophers you would have called us.

"That night was the last time I saw Frank. He went back to England a few months later. He left a note for me at the office and I would have gone to the quay to wish him well, but I had been sent to Port Elizabeth to cover some racial unrest down there and I was away the day his ship left. I was truly sorry I had missed him. We had got on well. And I didn't even have an address. The only place he had ever mentioned was Bristol."

~~~

Hugh, I think we should move from here.

But I know this place, it was where… it was where…

It was where you first saw me

Are you Barbara?

No, I am Nobomi. I don't know Barbara

I'm sorry

We must move away from here, so that you can leave these ghosts behind you. I believe that, Hugh. Now is the time. Listen and I will tell you a story from my ancestors. Are you listening? It starts in a village high on a plane just below a massive mountain. People called the mountain 'Dragon's Mountain'. When you took me to that hostel place to live, you remember, and we sat looking out of the big window all those afternoons, when I was sitting there I thought I could see the dragon's mountain and the plane below it, way beyond the city, and on the plane a little village called Matatiele. That is where this story starts. So please listen, Hugh. The village was poor because the people had been wandering for many years because of wars between tribes but in the end they found this place where there was just enough grass for their cows and the ground could grow enough food for the people and so they set up their homesteads and kraals and stopped wandering. Among them was a man and a woman, who had three daughters and the eldest was called Nobomi, like me, which means Life. After a few years a missionary came to the place and he started a school with his wife. They were white and not everyone wanted to mix with them or go to school, but Nobomi's parents wanted their children to learn more than just about growing food and herding cows, so they sent them to the school and they started to learn English. And soon the missionary saw that Nobomi was especially clever and he arranged for her to go to the nearest town where there was a bigger school. She was quite lost at first, because there were more people than she had ever seen before. And there were men in uniform with guns and that scared her. But she did well at her new school and she became very interested in all the new things and she saw that everywhere you go, there's always somewhere else to go and more new things, and on and on, perhaps for ever. When Nobomi went back to her family in their little village she saw that her parents were getting older and did not have enough for their three daughters, and her father did not have a son to provide for them, so she decided that because she was the oldest, she should leave and go somewhere where she could make her own life and perhaps she would even be able to send something back to help her family. She consulted an old seer in her village, where she should go, and this seer told her to go down to the Ocean where there were big towns and ships which went to other countries. And the seer pointed in the direction of the Ocean. One morning before anyone woke up Nobomi left. But it was much further than she thought and it took her almost two years to reach the Ocean. On the way she had been held captive on a farm and had to escape at night through a window, she had been chased by wild dogs and even shot at by a soldier who thought she was stealing, but in the end she arrived at a place called East London. She remembered the missionary had told her about London and she thought this might be a good place to make her new life. She wanted to send news back to her family, so she went to a Post Office where a young English man was very helpful and sent her telegraph for nothing. But her troubles were not over because she was staying with some men of her own tribe who did bad things to her one night and she had to escape again. She managed to find the man from the Post Office and he let her stay with him, because now she had no money at all. They fell in love, Hugh, and Nobomi became pregnant and she had a daughter and called her Ngoxolo, which means Peace. Hugh, Hugh, her daughter was my mother. And her father's name was Harry. Hugh, Harry was my grandfather.

Harry… so Harry was a long time ago, and you come from Harry… I didn't tell them… I never told them…

I kept you safe…

Yes, you did, Hugh. Thank you.

from the author's journal…

Everywhere we tread we leave a trace, a footprint which is indelibly ours, even though it manifests in as many forms and with as many superficies as the surfaces on which it's pressed… a deep indentation on the beach where the tide has just withdrawn, a sodden clarty mould of terra not quite firma, a dry and crusty imprint like a jacaranda pod, the shadow of a scuff on dusty bedrock – traces all of where we touched, or when a word of ours was heard or action felt, some veiled rebirthing, a name lost and found, ethereal DNA.

hope again…

John

Isn't so much of life down to happenstance?

I shouldn't have been here at all – Vienna, I mean – but in a weird coincidental way you could say there were connections in my life that made it, perhaps, appropriate. I suppose. The connections? Only one, really, at least that I knew about then, and that was that my father was a psychologist and he had been the first to write about what they now call post-traumatic stress, but then he called it shell-shock. He had been at the front in France in the First War and was the first to keep diary records of the soldiers they thought were cowards. He tried to stop them getting executed. Lieutenant CS Myers, Royal Army Medical Corps, that was my father.

And then… it was a coincidence that it was my stint in the hostel at all the week they came in, this fellow in a dirty military greatcoat, English, early thirties, with an African girl, a bit better dressed, younger, eighteen maybe. He seemed to have the bearing of a soldier, but he was emaciated and haggard. It was the girl who was holding things together for them.

Mariana, who was in charge of the nurses, one of those fearsome matrons with a heart of gold she tried not to let you see – she had had to do all the recruiting herself when she had arrived as a delegate from a Quaker relief mission and discovered that there were no care staff in the place – well, she caught me as I arrived that morning to tell me about this couple, who were causing some consternation. They were, to say the least, slightly unusual as a couple. He was a soldier, or had been, the girl said he had been a British officer. That raised difficult questions immediately – he was in a mess, so why had the army not looked after him, or was he a deserter? And the girl was black, seemingly from somewhere in the south of Africa – she said her family came from a place called Matatiele, but I had no idea where that was. She spoke good English and German, as well as what I presumed was her native language. I am sure I don't need to tell you that you didn't see African girls in Vienna in those days. How did she get here and how did she come to be with an older ex-British officer? But it wasn't this that was causing Mariana such concern as much as the mystery about their situation and his serious mental state. They had arrived late the previous evening – yes, Mariana had been on duty since then – and it was the girl who spoke for them. She said her name was Nobomi and the man's name was Hugh and they had been turned out of the cellar they had been occupying and needed shelter. The hostel had a small room which was being used for storage, so they put them in there, it had a bed and a chair, that was about all, no heating of course. It was down a couple of corridors and as they were coming to it, Mariana noticed the girl starting to look worried and unsure, and then, when they went in and Mariana had closed the door so she could sort things out, the man became hysterical and started screaming and clawing at the walls, he had looked as if he was going to hurt himself, but eventually after a quarter-hour or so he had huddled down on the floor in a corner sobbing. Mariana thought that she had stayed calm – it goes with her religion I am sure – but she admitted to me that she had been scared. But the girl, she couldn't believe. She said that the girl had talked quietly to him all the time, though you could barely hear above his screaming, and was saying something like "there's no-one here to hurt you Hugh" over and over, and then when his hysteria finally subsided and he was sitting sobbing in the corner, she just sat down beside him on the floor, her head bowed on her knees like his, and stayed completely still. After a while she managed to get him to lie on the bed and he fell asleep.

Mariana was amazed and she asked the girl, "How did you do that?" And the girl had just said, "I think we are connected, but I don't know how." That was all.

After Mariana had recounted all that, I just felt out of my depth. You see I'm not really a psychologist like my father. I've listened to him and read the diaries he kept about shell-shock and even read some of his papers from the Psychology Journal he started, but that's all. I only come to be here because the Quaker relief organisation wanted someone to come out and organise supplies and liaison generally for them in the city: they had heard there was only Mariana and she couldn't look after the staff and all the supplies and negotiation as well. And they thought it might be good to have a man about the place, because it wasn't a smart part of the city and if you had food coming in you were a target. There were still so many people going hungry in Vienna, you see. Then someone mentioned my father was a psychologist, so they had me down as the doctor as well. But I'm not a doctor and right now, I'm out of my depth.

Mariana said I must do something because if that happened regularly we would have trouble from the concierge of the block and the staff would get scared and leave. So I went to their room. The man was asleep on the bed and the girl was sitting alongside. I asked the girl to come out of the room with me so that we could talk, but she calmly refused. It was the way she said it, I suppose, it left me feeling, well, naked. I know that sounds strange, but it's the best way I can describe it. I had nothing. I had to start again. All she had said was, "I will not leave him." But it had such finality.

You should not think she was uncooperative, though. She told me everything she could in answer to my questions. First about their circumstances. Hugh had been in the British Army. He had found her one day in Stephansplatz and then another day had rescued her when a building collapsed. He had found a hostel for her and she had lived there for 3 years. He had visited every day to begin with, but then he had to go away and she had not seen him again until she found him like this one afternoon on a bench in Stephansplatz. That was about two years later. She said she did not know where he had been or what had happened to him, but she had arranged a cellar for them to sleep in and every day they went to the square and she would go and find them some food and when evening came they went back to the cellar. She did not seem perturbed, she simply said that Hugh was going to get better and then they would go to the land of her ancestors.

"Many things are connected which we do not know." I noticed her eyes sparkling.

One day a nice English lady had sat down by them in the square, she said, and had recognised the locket she always wore. "She told me what the picture was inside, and I had never shown anyone the locket except Hugh. I did not understand, but she knew that there was a man called Harry, who had lived near my ancestors' land and who was my grandfather. Often when he is upset and frightened Hugh seems to be in another place and someone is shouting at him, 'Harry, Lieutenant Winters, we want to know about Harry', and they must have been nasty and cruel to him because Hugh would shake. But he never told them. He never gave me away."

I would have asked more, but I thought that was enough for a beginning. I told Nobomi to open the door when Hugh was awake and when one of the staff came past to ask them to come and tell me and I would come back.

I sat in our office and tried to make the story work in my head, the unwavering certainty of the girl and the implausibility of what she had just told me. I reminded myself of what I once heard my father say, "You don't have to accept as truth all that the patient says, but you must accept as your certainty that what you have heard is the patient's truth."

The hours were passing and there was no word from the room. Mariana seemed less perturbed now – I think because the risk of disturbance to the air of peace she sought to maintain was reduced, which I was afraid might mean she had a faith in my competence that I did not have myself. When the time for our midday meal was approaching, I decided to visit our new residents even though I had had no call. As I approached their door, I was concerned in case unexpected intrusion might be enough to set off the man's distress, but I knocked quietly and the girl came to the door and let me in. She said that he had part woken several times, but never into a state where he could understand a new situation. Now he was asleep, but from time to time you could see a writhing torment on his face. The girl herself seemed quite subdued. It could simply have been a weariness from lack of sleep, of course, but her eyes certainly did not have the sparkle they had when she was telling me about the English lady in Stephansplatz. I decided to turn my attention to her, since her man was so comatose. Her man?

"No, we are not together in that way."

"Would you explain for me?"

"My people have a saying – I am because you are – and it is like that for Hugh and me. When Hugh is not well, I cannot feel the same person. It is friend's love, but it does not mean sex. It is more important to be like this.

"What is your name, doctor?"

"My name is John, but I am not a doctor. That is, I am not a medical doctor. My father was a psychologist in the army in the First War and I have learnt from him. He was the first person to make sense of what happens to people when they have been through things so bad that their brains cannot cope and they cannot be with others like ordinary people can. They become like your friend Hugh. They are ill and they don't get better unless they have the right people with them, people who are patient and know how to help them."

"Will you be able to do that for Hugh?"

"I will be able to help a little. But I think you will help him more than me."

"I am scared when he is like he was last night."

"That is natural, to be scared when someone is so distressed and screaming. But Mariana said you were very calm."

"I am not scared of **his** screaming. I know that I am here to help him back to life." She paused head bowed. "I am scared of the scream in me." She looked up, as if searching for an answer.

"You have these dreadful times as well?"

"I don't know where the scream is. I don't know who is screaming. The sound seems far away, but the fear is very close. It holds me with its claws. Mbulu."

"Is it there now?"

"Yes."

In that moment I realised I had not one patient, but two.

"How did you come here, to Vienna?"

Long moments passed. Then, whispered, "I don't know."

The man stirred, attempting to rise, straightaway she turned for him and Fear's hold was broken. For now.

Not wanting to risk stress for the man, waking with another person in the room I left, so that Nobomi could explain who I was and that she would like him to talk to me, and then to arrange for that later in the day. I was careful to make certain one of the staff would stay on that corridor in the meantime and listen out for any disturbance. Then I went off to eat.

~~~

"I didn't understand what they wanted. It wasn't what they should have wanted. They should have wanted to know all the people who were in that strike committee meeting because one of them had betrayed the movement to the police to stop the revolt, which would mean the Russians wouldn't come over. I could have told them who they were, but they didn't ask. They just wanted Harry, and there wasn't a Harry. I didn't know a Harry. I wasn't brave. I wanted to help them, but I couldn't. I suppose I should have told them anything. No, they would have killed me. I said that once, "Just kill me, I can't tell you, I don't know, so just kill me." It would have been alright. To kill me. No use to them. But they kept me going. Every day. Same time. Important. Once he was late. I started to feel panic. I walked round and round my cell. Started to shake. I screamed. I hit the wall. They'd taken away my life, but they hadn't killed me. The panic was tearing me apart. But then I heard him somewhere behind. I heard him say – 'we're late'. And it was ok. I was safe."

Don't think that was that first afternoon. No, I had spent several periods talking to Hugh, with Nobomi at his side, but they were all me talking, and rather ineptly too, so I am not going to re-tell those here. This was the first afternoon that Hugh had given anything back, and without my asking, he had just started. To my relief he had also given me a clue and I could now have Nobomi play a part in his cure. Yes, I was still hoping I might find a cure. Hugh was no longer to be left to wake or sleep at will, but she would rouse him at the same time each morning and she would take him out and walk the same route with him every day – we were lucky there was a park just across the road – for half an hour exactly. And after a few days she would do it twice a day, but always at the same times every day.

I heard my father again – "Listen, not just to the words, but to what has meaning for your patient." I felt a sigh of relief… and in my mind I thanked Hugh for his clue.

Nobomi was absolutely meticulous in following my instructions. Each morning at 10 exactly they went out of the front of the hostel, crossed the road and went into the park. I saw them as they disappeared down one of the avenues, not hand in hand like lovers, but like two people who felt comfortable and safe with each other and for whom the other was important. Occasionally Nobomi would look at Hugh and he would look at her and they exchanged some words, but I suspect that mostly they walked in silence, the two of them sharing a view which I hoped, even briefly, for both of them, might not be blighted by sinister shadows. At 10.30 exactly they returned.

As the days and weeks go by, the therapist – I suppose I should call myself that, since I couldn't lay claim to any formal qualification – the therapist notices his anxiety increasing, even if his patient is doing well. With the improving patient he is increasingly concerned that they don't leave his care too soon, spurred on by their growing confidence, and have a relapse; with the patient who continues to suffer, the therapist's anxiety is focused on his own competence and the possibility that something may have been missed, which might risk the patient's chances of recovery. Remember that at this time we lacked the benefit of systematic studies and research into the after-effects of trauma – my father's 'shell-shock' – or even in many cases the means of identifying the symptoms of exposure to brutal experiences. And so it was for me, a hovering anxiety, as well as a growing unease for which I could find no specific cause. Nobomi's steady advancing of Hugh's programme had never been interrupted, and most days Hugh had been able to spend a short period with me at which I simply invited him to talk about what was in his mind. At first those quarter-hour sessions were with Nobomi sitting with him, but after a couple of weeks he was even able to come alone. All was going well. So what was this nagging fear in me?

After a while I was able to talk to Nobomi alone as well, because Hugh could tolerate a half-hour without her. I was concerned about her for the sake of Hugh's recovery and I was also concerned for her own health because of those periods of fear which seemed to stalk her and grip her at unexpected times. And, I'll be honest, I was curious, and curiosity for its own sake is not an easy thing for a therapist to face up to – I had never spent time with a black person in any capacity, and in these circumstances I was interested in how the fact that her roots and culture were so different from my own would affect this work. More than that, though, I was interested to see how spending this time with her was going to affect me.

At first she would not respond when I asked her directly about her fear. But I was too direct. She just sat impassive, head bowed. "Slowly, gently, step by step" I heard my father say. I wondered aloud what was the last thing she could remember that wasn't Vienna. "Mbulu", she said quite suddenly. As she said the word she looked up at me and I saw that her eyes had lost the peaceful serenity they normally had, her body became rigid, her face was taut, her eyes wide open with a fearful stare.

"What is Mbulu?"

But she was not staring at me, she was looking way beyond, I could not imagine into what dark place. "Not fingers, claws", her face creased in horror, her hands lifted to try to blot out some image, then a scream like nothing I had ever heard before, "Nooooooooooooo….."

Extract from Port Elizabeth police investigation at Korsten, Eastern Cape, 4th September 1938

"I was sitting at the table by the window when it all started. You can see straight across the road to 56. Me alone that night, my sister 'ad gone out with her boy to drink, staying out probably. Me, have no boy now because the boy that was mine called Nkosi started beating me too much and I discarded him. There was no noise that night, I was thinking like it was too quiet. A white man comes to Nobomi's house, that's 56. The one who comes for her meetings. He went in. Her daughter was with this man. They looking all around, like they didn't want no-one to see them. They shut the door quickly when they're in. Nothing happened for one hour or more. Then a waggon arrives. I thought these are not workmen at this time of day. They took a big tree off the back, it was cut to a pole, four of them there were, big mans. They put the log down on the path in front of the door. The leader man, he was drunk, he starts to try to talk to the daughter through the door. I was not hearing what he was saying, but he was cursing her and she shouted, then that stopped. I thought that's it, all over. But it was not. Those men they picked up the log yelling and ran at the door and broke it down. These houses aren't strong. Keep the rain out, that's about it. This log beaten the door to pieces, and the frame, and twisted the zinc both sides. I saw everything inside. They were stamping on everything. Then I started to shake. I saw the leader man took the daughter to the floor and he climbed on her with one of those miner's small pick-axes and he's crashing in her head. Then blood shoot up all over. Then I hear a scream, it was a child, "Noooooooooo…….." seemed to go on and on, never heard nothing like that, hope I never do again. Then that big man that was many times there, was like her protector, ran up panting, grabbed the pick-axe and smashed the head of the leader man over and over. Or it may have been her. Nobomi. Too much to see. The other men running out. Then silence for a while. After that the big man came out with the daughter wrapped in a cloth. He had her over his shoulder. The white man carryin' the little child. I didn't see where he went. Then you lot arrived."

The scream brought Mariana running. She burst into the room, another carer in tow. I was relieved that she didn't immediately rush to comfort Nobomi. I had learnt we must beware not to rend the fragile tissue which holds a life together, just. There were other chairs around us and I motioned to the ladies to sit and together we waited, the four of us, a silent congregation, until Nobomi's vision faded.

~~~

"I remember when I was with the International Quakers in Vienna after the first war," – Mariana and I were sitting alone in the staff common room that evening after everything had gone quiet – "we had quite a mixture of people helping, we even had an English soldier in our block, as well as an English Quaker nurse. I think her name was Isabella. She was the most experienced of all of us because she had also been in South Africa during the

Boer Wars and had looked after the Boer families that the British had put into these communal camps when they wanted to clear the countryside. Mainly women and children and the conditions were very bad, very little food and often no clean water. She said that if you were lucky you had a building, but a lot were just tents, and over-crowded, a lot of disease. She was in the camp in East London, but that was closed down and then she went to somewhere near Johannesburg. Then almost 20 years later there she was in Vienna doing the same work. Mainly feeding people who were almost starving, but the houses that had a nurse were sent the people who needed more help. And the pregnant women! That's what Isabella was known for. Mid-wife, you say in English. I think I like it better how the French say it, wise-woman." An almost twinkling smile passes across Mariana's face and I realise that this is not something I have noticed before. Calm, serene, a little stern, these are the words you would use for this steady steward of the lives of our unfortunates, no visible uncertainty, no hesitation that could make you doubt your sanctuary, but then this glint in blue-grey eyes and she opens up and lets you glimpse… I wondered if that was Isabella too, but Mariana was there before me… "Isabella deserved that title, she was always the person at your side, smiling, made friends with everybody, all through her life. That was her reputation."

I mused about the lore of human existence which made of the 'weaker sex' the sustainers of the fabric of survival and of the 'stronger sex' the producers of the faults and tears which mar the weave and threaten its very cohesion. Until today you would have said that Nobomi and Hugh were playing these roles perfectly, each with their own part and keeping to their own script. From this point, though, the course of this drama seemed less certain, and for myself, as a bystander and occasional small part player, my uneasiness increased, for as much as I felt a little more confidence in my own contribution, there was growing in me what nowadays I would term an empathic sadness, a kind of resignation.

Over the next few days Mbulu, whatever Mbulu was or is, did not make an appearance. Neither was there an occasion during our talks that Nobomi seemed to come near to that distraught emotional state which had produced the scream. But I didn't believe it had gone for good and I wondered how long it would be before it would feel safe to step down that path again. Sometimes, though, the therapist only needs to follow. So it was in our next few sessions.

I learnt about a Xhosa girl, the eldest of three daughters who grew up in a tiny scattered village of round huts and kraals on a high plane in the shadow of the Drakensberg mountains, two hundred miles from the Ocean. Her parents had managed to bring the family this far from their homeland, after the Zulu had started a war against their clan, overrun their land and driven their people out. One of her sisters was very sick and they could go no further, but the local people were welcoming enough and so they settled, grew some food on the land around their home and her father was able to keep some cattle to support them. The place was called Matatiele, which means 'the ducks have flown away'. "I think that was because it was once a marsh, but then the land had dried," she explained, "and so the ducks left." The eldest daughter was clever. All three girls went to a mission school in the village, but after a year the eldest was sent to a better school in a town which she had to be taken to on horseback by her uncle, a journey which took them several days. She had to stay in the town while the school was open, but she went home when it closed and lived again with her family. Finally, she left the family home because her ageing father could not support all three girls, and she walked a very long way until she came to a big town by the Ocean. She lived there a while, but in the end she had to leave again. Only, now she had a baby daughter.

Now you will be confused if, like me, you thought that Nobomi was telling her own story.

"That Nobomi wasn't me, John. That Nobomi was my grandmother." She paused and seemed to be looking down a long passage.

"I think she was special. Our name means Life. She only had one man, and he died before my mother was born."

Then she looked straight into my eyes smiling, and added casually, "He was English, like you." I felt an indefinable stirring somewhere deep down inside.

Another pause, then quietly: "I think there was something more. I do wonder if there was ever another man. Perhaps I am going to find out. We are on our way to find her. We are going back to Matatiele when Hugh is strong. Perhaps I will see her again. And she will tell me more of the story. I was very young when I last saw her and she probably thought I would not understand. But now I can understand... and why the story stopped.

"It was my grandmother who told me about the Mbulu. At first I thought she was telling me an ancestor story, because my people often tell their children about the ancestors and they are good stories because the ancestors always want the children to be happy and healthy. But this wasn't one of those stories. Mbulu are really monsters for our people, John. But they are monsters who can look like people. You can tell a Mbulu if it has a tail, but they can hide their tails too and sometimes all you might see is that their hands are more like claws.

"My grandmother told me about a dream she often had where she was trying to get back to her home and her family at Matatiele and there were always Mbulu stopping her. There were black ones and white ones and they were fighting and she didn't know which were on her side. At the end of the dream she was on the shore of the Ocean and she was always completely alone.

"I think there was something else in the dream, but she wouldn't tell me what it was. I hope she will tell me one day. I hope it's alright now."

~~~

Our lives seemed to be falling into a regular pattern – I say 'our' because it felt at times that the combination of the regularity of activity which I had encouraged intentionally for Hugh and Nobomi and the fact that my time with the two of them had a rhythm which none of my other work in the hostel afforded, that all of this gave a feeling of our being a unit, the three of us, in a way. Perhaps it was not as comfortable as that might sound – certainly there were pressures, not least from Mariana – and perhaps I was allowing this beginner therapist's antennae to lose their sensitive tuning, lulled by the very regularity which I saw as part of the therapeutic process. Mariana became concerned that we should not be using resources to support clients who appeared increasingly able to support themselves – there was always more demand for services than there were the means to meet it. I prickled at what I felt as her intrusion into my domain, but nonetheless was forced to consider whether this was needful concern or a novice's over-compensation, which I was allowing to rule my judgment.

The first sign of a wobble came from Hugh. They returned early from their morning walk one day. It had extended now to over an hour, but that morning they came back well before the hour and not side by side as they usually were, rather with Hugh out in front striding in the disordered way of someone very perturbed. Nobomi was a few steps behind looking upset and bewildered. Later in the day she said that she thought he had been in a low mood since the previous evening and that morning had not spoken at all. They had started on their walk and in the middle of the park had sat down at his instigation on a bench and he had remained like that, his head in his hands, for several minutes. When he looked up he had caught sight of a man and a woman sitting under an ornamental canopy not far away, they were at one of the refreshment tables and drinking tea. His body had gone rigid as if suddenly frozen in time and then tears came into his eyes and ran down his cheeks and he appeared to be in a trance. After a few minutes he had got up and almost like a train gathering speed had set off back to the hostel. She had only been able to follow on behind him, ever quickening her pace, realising that she did not exist in whatever world he had found himself.

I trusted Nobomi to know how she could find a way back into Hugh's world and help him to return to ours. So it was the afternoon before I went to find him to have our usual exchange. I found him calm but very downcast. Nobomi quietly left the room.

"I must have thought it was Barbara," he began, "it didn't come to me when I saw them, I've worked it out since. How could it have been Barbara? – she was with a man so I would have been looking at myself. And it wasn't sudden jealousy, I didn't really see the man, only what they were doing, drinking tea." He smirked. "Coffee probably. It was my head making it up, wasn't it? Making what I saw to be Barbara and me."

I had learnt the name of Barbara from a previous conversation, but only as a passing reference to a girlfriend from another time. Now, though, she was a real presence, a longed-for painful presence.

"I ruined her life. Barbara. I was waiting to go back and have tea with her in Bath, my last few days in the army, when the Russians lifted me and slung me into that vile black hole. She'd given up a marriage to be there for me. Because I promised. She had no way back… and she must have waited and waited… in a caravan!… and I never came. I broke my promise."

"Was there ever any other way?"

"I started it. I was having tea and I asked her to sit down at my table. And there was I, I was going back off leave that night. Selfish tinpot soldier. Yes, there was another way."

"Perhaps…"

"And risk doing more damage? I have enough to condemn myself already. I can never be a man of honour again. It was still a war and I didn't see it. Some men have no choice, have to bring their woman into their war. I had a choice. My war wasn't Barbara's war. She had already fought hers. She drove ambulances through the blitz… no bomb ever fell near me."

His delivery was slow, though more resigned than maudlin, as if he were trudging down a road with no turnings to an end in no man's land.

My father had told me that some of his patients never recovered, and even some who seemed to, did not survive. He thought that the sustained effect of physical suffering that could not be comprehended, was to permanently distort the schemes of reasoning which our minds use to function in a recognisable world.

Suicide can follow torture, even long after. I feared for Hugh's life.

Nobomi also seemed shaken. We had been sitting, mostly in silence, that evening in an upstairs room, a general-purpose room which the carers sometimes used for resting between duties. It was in a mansard roof-space and had windows looking out over the city.

"When I was in the mission for girls on Alsergrund, Hugh came every afternoon and we would just sit looking out over the city like this. I believed that along the hazy line where the sky and the land meet, I could see my homeland. I believed that one day I would get back there. And Hugh would have to be with me. I think he knew that. I hope he still knows that, even though his homeland is somewhere else."

She paused, her head tilted to one side.

"I want everything to be connected so that in the end it can all work out. I suppose it always does work out. In the end. In some way. I think there will be a link between Hugh and me, not relations I don't mean, I don't think that is possible, but don't we all meet so many people, and each of those meet so many others and so on and on… somewhere along all those winding paths there will be a way to find everyone?"

She looked across at me.

"Louie. I haven't told you everything about Louie. Another time."

With that she got up and said, "I must go and find Hugh."

At least, I thought, the day's events will allow me a little leeway with Mariana and her insistence that people should move on as soon as they had the means.

~~~

It was a few weeks later that Mariana took the opportunity of our being alone together to reveal another side of her concerns about Hugh and Nobomi.

"I know that you have a feel for Vienna with the wide variety of people we see here, but you don't have the sort of feel for the place which comes from living in the city in the bad times. Vienna has had some very bad times. Not just what people know about on the surface, but underneath as well. And even though our new government is telling us that we have our country back and are free from the occupation and all its evils, we cannot yet know whether things have really changed."

It was clear that this conversation had a purpose.

"I know, especially being English, that you will feel strongly your commitment to your patient's confidentiality. I admire the English and the way you are so professional, but how much do you know about Hugh during his time in our city? How much do you *really* know?"

I felt the embarrassment of the naïve schoolboy who had not thought through the consequences of his actions. I managed not to project my discomfort onto Mariana who, despite her matronly manner, was seeking to point to her concern in an uncritical and constructive way.

"And if it comes that you have concerns outside the therapy you administer, will you make me aware?"

She looked uncertain, but continued, indicating why she had brought this up now. "The other day one of the carers came to me. She said that she had often been in a room upstairs on the front to help the resident there and it was the time Hugh and Nobomi went out for their walk. She could see them in the park and she thought they were usually followed. During the occupation we were used to recognising the various undercover types, they could be police, militia, contacts of the intelligence of all four militaries, our own secret police, but she did not think this man – always the same man – was any of those."

"I am worried," she went on, "because there are many things which could be dangers for our work and for our clients. Our freedoms as a country are very new and now the occupation troops are leaving there are many people who want to settle scores and take revenge. And perhaps we have not changed so much – there is still much Nazi way of thinking – how many black people do you see in Vienna? Hugh is badly damaged but someone might still think he is a risk, do you know for certain it was the Russians who tortured him? – he was not sent to Moscow for execution, he did not end in the gulags…"

I could not brush away Mariana's questions. I had to admit that I could not know. What can we ever *really* know? But that's a lofty philosophical question and we were living the aftermath of a city's tortured past, the grime and the guilt in with the glory. "…accept as your certainty that what you have heard is the patient's truth…", but therapy exists in the world, Father.

No, I had no answer.

"I will start to talk about how they leave and where they go next, Mariana."

"Thank you."

~~~

Nobomi did not seem surprised that I was wanting to talk about where they might move from here. Hugh seemed indifferent, which itself caused me concern. I was having a joint talk with them, something we had started to do over the last couple of weeks. I sensed in Nobomi a yearning to be away from the confinement of the city – she was after all a child of open spaces, at least to the extent that I was able to imagine her homeland. At this point perhaps I should confess that one afternoon when my services were not needed I had visited the library in Felderstrasse – not too far from here in the Town Hall buildings – to see if I could find the place where "the ducks have flown away". After a lot of searching through indexes and enormous leather-bound atlases with pages as big as newspapers, some interleaved with fine semi-transparent india-paper, I found it. Matatiele. It seemed to be on its own in the middle of an area of green-brown shading on the map. Just to the north wound a wide band of grey, light in places but dark grey along a central thread with snaking blue rivers intersecting. I worked out it must have stretched some 600 miles in all. Its name, one word, wove along its length: Drakensberg. With the help of an old Dutch dictionary I worked out that it meant Dragon's Mountain. I was in South Africa. Words like Eastern Cape and Basuto and KwaZulu were lying around and cities I only knew as names, Johannesburg, Durban, Cape Town. East London caught my eye, perhaps because it sounded a little incongruous, perhaps because on this sheet it lay on the coast above the cartographer's florid inscription of 'Indian Ocean'. I looked around again to find Matatiele, a long way inland, and wondered what it had been like for a teenage Xhosa country girl from the mountains to walk well over 100 miles to the Ocean and arrive at a European town called East London. The Nobomi I hadn't met. Yet.

I've digressed. I hope your imagination is not inventing any unseemly sub-conscious promptings. I was going to lose my clients and I was floundering, partly from professional concern and partly, well, lives which had been part of my life were about to disappear. It is human to want to keep a connection. We rarely simply walk away.

They were both in our meeting that afternoon and I managed to prompt Hugh to give the same sort of account of his stress episode to the three of us as he had done to me on my own previously. The fact that he went there so easily was both a comfort and a worry, but I was hoping to use his openness to lead into a shared discussion on how they would handle such episodes together in the future, for they would certainly happen again. I wanted Nobomi to hear about the result of sustained senseless suffering and its indelible effect on Hugh's thinking and reactions, such as the insidious infiltration of self-blame and 'just deserts', the unpredictability and vulnerability which may stay with him always, the ever-present possibility of suicide. At the same time, I was conscious that it all seemed a monstrous burden to place on one who had her own 'evil spirit' lurking – that Fear with claws, which caused her to scream. Hugh was composed and considerate now, archetypal British officer-class, but always willing to admit that, yes, depression could come upon him. He seemed to believe he could rely on his voice of reason to talk him through the trough when the need arose, but I was afraid that he was unable to recognise that he could lose this self-control in an instant, unexpectedly, unforeseen and unaware, and the impenetrable black mist descend again. For him, the quiet, unquestioning, patient, presence of this girl whose name meant Life, who walked so lightly on the earth and seemed to see beyond horizons, was the best therapist he could ever have. For Nobomi, though, there would not be the same security, and this thought cut through me like a blade. Where lies the true therapist's responsibility? The master might tell his new practitioner – this is only one and you have many more, equally deserving, who are waiting.

Yes, but in each single moment there *is* only one.

I chose not to mention the man who had been seen following them on their walks. Speaking to you now, I can still feel the swing between anxiety and complacency as I try to decide the right course. But I did not tell them.

In the end I found myself wondering who was preparing who for the parting. Hugh was steady and I concluded that his bouts of severe depression were set off by random sightings or events, which I thought might be as little as a turn of phrase in a particular tone of voice, but being random could not be predicted, or part of any cycle. To construct a life around un-knowable happenstance was inconceivable. Nobomi seemed concerned for me, as if the course of my life had somehow become connected with their's… or hers? I had told her nothing of myself and I wondered whether our unit of three, this place, Vienna, and my therapist persona had become fused as an entity, and with others took its place somewhere on the open plane of her homeland which she seemed to carry always with her. Perhaps that was as it should be.

I didn't see them leave the last time. We had come together the previous evening, the three of us up in that mansard room looking out over the lights of the city. The midnight blue of a clear night sky allowed the horizon to be just discernible like the marker of another world. We each knew the meaning and the ritual of this gazing over the city and we spoke very little. The following morning I called at their room because I needed to re-arrange the time for our meeting that day, but the room was bare.

Mariana said that one of the staff had told her she saw them go out on their walk earlier than usual and the man who followed them was there as always, but this time, she couldn't be sure, but she thought he was walking between them as they went out of sight through the trees in the park.

A yawning emptiness opened up inside me. I went out of the building and walked aimlessly into the park, scanning the cruelly ordered paths and lawns, as if... as if, what?

No, Father, she wasn't just a patient.

part two

THE EASTERN PROVINCE HERALD, PORT ELIZABETH, CAPE OF GOOD HOPE.

MONDAY, OCTOBER 25, 1920.

TERRIBLE CALAMITY IN CITY

TRAGIC END TO NATIVE RIOT

POLICE FIRE ON DENSE CROWD

FEARFUL PANIC REIGNS

BAAKENS STREET A SHAMBLES

DEATH-ROLL TOTALS 23

SCORES OF PERSONS WOUNDED

NIGHT ATTACKS ON CITY OUTSKIRTS

Stark tragedy was the outcome on Saturday of the native agitation which has been simmering for the past few weeks.

Late in the afternoon, following on determined attacks made by a great mob of armed natives on the Police Station, Constables, assisted by returned soldiers, who were defending the Court House opened fire with rifles. Ghastly scenes followed wherein men, and in some cases women, fell before the bullets of the defenders and the kerries of the frenzied natives.

A night of great anxiety followed with the City wearing the aspect of an armed camp. And in the early hours of the morning there were one or two other encounters between the organised patrols and bands of natives armed with a miscellany of weapons who were openly bent on mischief.

117

INCEPTION OF THE TROUBLE

That trouble was brewing in less responsible native quarters has been evident to most people for some time. Primarily – the unrest has been due to those economic causes which in later years have proved so unsettling a factor throughout the world. But there is no manner of doubt that unscrupulous agitators amongst the natives have deliberately set themselves to foster and aggravate a sense of wrong.

For some time now an organisation styling itself the Industrial and Commercial (Amalgamated) Coloured and Native Workers' Union has been in being. It is to this organisation that is directly attributable the deplorable events of Saturday,. Its leaders have conducted a campaign in which the preaching of much-perverted trades union doctrines have played a principal part. Violent and inflammatory speech has been freely indulged in, and there is no doubt that the organisers attracted to their ranks a large body not only of the irresponsible young bloods and the rawer elements of the native population, but also a predominating proportion of the rowdy, tough, and criminal classes. With this combustible ready and eager to believe whatever was told to it, trouble was bound to ensue at an earlier or later date.

The chief factor in the organisation appears to have been a native of some personality named Masabalala. He figured as the president and issued edicts in the name of the Union.

EXTRAVAGANT DEMANDS

It has apparently been one of his objects to inculcate the idea that the native when organised is competent to demand whatever wage he may think fit. This naturally appealed strongly to the classes from which his followers were drawn. Thus it will doubtless be recollected that a couple of months back an advertisement was published notifying all employers, industrial, commercial and domestic, that henceforth the rate of pay for native males was to be ten shillings and sixpence per day and for native females seven shillings and sixpence per day.

In recent weeks it has been evident that the organisation was desirous of precipitating a crisis doubtless with an eye to possible prestige to be gained therefrom. Thus it has been noticeable that recently the efforts of the agitators have been intensified with the result that a lawless spirit has sprung up and developed. A great deal of violent speech has been indulged in whilst open intimidation has been practised in respect of those native workers who do not see eye to eye with the members of the Union, Such threats as that to be beaten to death with sticks have been conveyed to peaceable workers of both sexes, and it has clearly been the intention to terrify all sections of the natives into co-operating in the Union's ambitious desire of a general native strike.

Let me say straightaway, so that you don't get the wrong opinion of me, that I did not write that editorial. I had been there at Baakens Street police station, I had a young rookie with me – he was scared out of his wits when the shooting started, so would I have been if I hadn't been making sure we caught everything we needed – and we got some good angles, I even managed to take down some of the talk and at one point we got around the back and got a picture of the volunteers going into the police station with rifles – they were going up to shoot from the balcony – but we had to run for our lives once they spotted we had cameras. Anyway, I had submitted stories and pictures when we got back, but they were all withdrawn by the boss before the edition went to press – he said there wasn't time to get all the plates made, but that wasn't it. He had got one of the subs to read my stuff and then write a one-sided account which said nothing at all about the real causes. That is what you have just read.

It was a sad day. Port Elizabeth is a segregated city, well, we call it a city, you would probably call it a town, but nothing like this had ever happened before. The crowd had been building all afternoon to 400 or more I would say. And in the end more again. It had been orderly, noisy but orderly, Africans are used to waiting. I'm not sure what started it off. There was a line of armed police, about 20 of them, along the verandah, and they were standing impassive like a wall, glaring out from their vantage positions. We were on the fringe on the higher side of the road and I think there was a surge in the middle of the crowd, just numbers I'm sure and someone stumbled, no more than that, but the surge looked like a whirlpool which was being propelled towards the front, and then there was a shot. A single shot. A moment of total silence. A scream. Then chaos. More shots, coming from the balcony, I'm sure. The crowd now like a sea with eddies which formed and then opened up and in the depths you could just see contorted figures, sometimes still, sometimes writhing. Spaces then as the crowd scattered, up the

street, round corners, behind walls, until the road was
deserted and bare, except for these heaps of fabric with
brown and black extensions of hands and heads, and hats
scattered, and dark pools of blood.

23 were killed, 20 black and 3 coloureds – yes, the crowd
had been mixed, though mainly native African – and 50
injured, except they won't all have been counted.
Shameful.

I cried.

The town was divided of course – interests, politics, class,
colour – but don't think it was simple. You could say that
the non-Whites in towns like ours had bought into the
colonial system – I imagine others in their number might
say "sold out" – because it could give them jobs and
property and houses and a position. You might hear that it
all started with the cattle-killing last century, a hysteria set
off by a seer among the Xhosa, and tens of thousands of
them moved to the towns from the country to avoid
starvation. The towns needed them because development
and expansion were held back by lack of labour, so both
sides won, you could say. For a few that happened. There
started to be black professionals and landlords and
businesses, a black middle-class, though nothing like as
well-paid or well-off as the whites of course. But the
whites started to get nervous, just the numbers for a start,
and owning property, and not behaving in the same way
as they did, not having past generations of 'civilisation and

education' – you can see what I mean. And most Africans expected their children to be educated in the European way, and they dressed like whites, and wanted to be 'respectable' middle class. And then the whites got even more worried. And scared.

So here we are. 23 dead. An intelligent educated popular leader – Masabalala was his name, the editorial got that right – was trying to get an increase for the factory and shore workers, whose two shillings and sixpence a week – no, the editorial didn't get that right – wouldn't feed them after the price increases from the war. The police thought that taking him into custody would tame the crowd. Of course, it didn't. The crowd still waited. Another two hours. The tension was growing, you could feel it. In the end it was so high that something was surely going to set it off. And then the police decided there was nothing left to do but shoot. But the rioting and the marches went on in and around the city.

Needless to say, the police got the upper hand over the next few days and then the authorities could come in offering negotiations – so magnanimous (you will notice that sometimes I resort to the English humour of sarcasm) – but these were the sort of negotiations which gave away only a miserly amount. The Africans still couldn't live, not if they had a family anyway. But the authorities got a payback they didn't expect, because a lot of the Africans left the town and went back to the country, and then there wasn't enough cheap labour for the port and industry.

"That's Justice", I wanted to write, but I'm not allowed to be political, or only on one side. After that weekend a few of my colleagues who knew that the boss had pulled my editorial and substituted the biased one you've read, told me I had better keep my head down for a bit if I wanted to keep my job.

Things got a bit quieter anyway, but there was still discontent simmering below the surface. And real suffering for a lot of families. You knew things would blow up somewhere eventually. But it took a while, and now I wasn't allowed to go near any reporting which I might use to make an issue. I lost my rookie assistant and got given all the routine jobs. To be honest I lost my drive and just drifted along, a bit like at the Dispatch after Mr Crosby left. So I was back to the hack stuff, you might say. Hmm, a bit pompous, put like that, but here I was, I'd moved down from the Dispatch and I was no further on than when I started years ago.

Face it Adam, you lose heart and get set in your ways.

You know how it is, you get too comfortable and that seems to take away the incentive to move on and make something of yourself, and then you start making excuses like you're waiting for the right opportunity to come up. In a way it did happen like that, when I was at the Dispatch. I applied to the Cape Times, but I didn't get the job – not a wide enough range of reporting experience, they said. That hurt. Why did it hurt? Well, imagine you had pioneered something new in your trade, and then you were turned down like that. Photo-reporting was my thing. When I first went to the Dispatch, I had been given the latest camera gear and the boss said he wanted me to be photographer and reporter in one, take the shots to be a moving picture record of the story as I wrote it. "And I don't want the usual trite rubbish people want to tell you so that they look good," he would say, "dig, dig, dig, and let your camera help you, I don't care how much film you use, keep shooting and then you'll capture what things *mean* to people, that's what we want to print, what it means, not what the mayor, the council, the police, the bosses, the health inspector, the magistrate, not what they all want it to *look* like. Go through your images, look at the expressions on people's faces, and if you see something that could be a story in a story, go back and take another look." He was out on his own, Mr Crosby. A genuine revolutionary in these parts. But he retired and the directors softened his approach. Had me in once and told me I had to tone it down. That's when I started looking elsewhere. Cape Town was the obvious place, the Cape Times, you couldn't do better. But like I said, they rejected me, saying 'not enough experience', though really I think they were worried about antagonising the State government.

So here I am at the Eastern Province Herald. Half-way house you might say, but Port Elizabeth is bigger than East London and is more liberal. Or so they think. But now I've been silenced. I'm ashamed to say it was a few years before I woke up again and even then I almost missed it.

Weddings! Yes, that's what they gave me. I could sleep-walk them. If you'd seen me, you'd probably have said I *was* sleep-walking them. But in the end, I was glad I was given this one. Couldn't see it at the time though. It should have occurred to me that black weddings don't get covered by a reporter-photographer unless the bridegroom is a little bit notable. So I should have at least looked up who he was before I got to the church. I knew the significance as soon as I read the notes of course, because it was Themba Wauchope, who was one of the nephews of Isaac Wauchope – his uncle had been involved in the wrangle with the municipality and the government over freehold rights for natives building in the New Brighton Location back in 1905. Themba's bride was an unknown, a local told me, a Xhosa girl, whose mother had come from up towards Basuto. When I saw her, the bride I mean, I couldn't put that together, because she didn't look like a Xhosa from the far country, especially not right up in the Drakensberg. Small breasts, less rounded figure – please excuse a man's observations, but it's the reporter's instinct to notice. I didn't know much about the bridegroom, other than he had got involved over the attempts to apply the Pass regulations in the city and was in the ANC. But everyone knew of his uncle, the Reverend Isaac, though he had been dead 5 years now.

So, a wedding people would want to read about, but I still didn't see where I was going to find that 'meaning' old Crosby was always on about, at a conventional middle-class wedding in Korsten, even though Korsten was the Location the council had never managed to rule. The 'meaning', when I finally got it, became something very personal. So was it in the paradox of a probably very impoverished country girl marrying into a respected, almost revered, African family? That was off the mark by quite a long way. It was something I didn't spot until I was going through the photos back in the office the next day. I had had to take the usual families photos, everybody arranged in stiff lines – I hate them – but it was in one of these that I noticed the bride's mother in a striking black and white dress. I was fairly sure I had seen her before, but not from the dress or even her overall appearance, more her look, the way she was gazing out, like she was viewing a distant horizon. I had seen that look before. I had *photographed* that look before. But not here and not recently. East London? The shadow of a memory flickered in my mind.

It would be a while longer before that memory became clear. And it would be a very different sort of story, but the puzzle was enough to make me want to start digging, even if I had to do it in my own time.

The reporter's instinct was back. And I was relieved.

~~~

I've found that newcomers to Cape Province and particularly to Port Elizabeth are quite puzzled by the contrasts and contradictions which they find. They don't expect to find Jews like me among the locals for a start, but that's another story. They step off the boat and they see the town stretching up the hillside from the wide bay, and looking quite like some coastal town in northern Europe, one of the channel ports, perhaps. Isn't the architecture along sea fronts much the same anywhere? because their town councils want to look grand for visitors? Here it's spoilt a bit in places because so much of the Port work happens on the shore, not being a river port like East London. But as they venture away from the sea-front the visitors start to notice that stone often gives way to wood for building – not the important civic buildings and stores of course, but off the main street, and the further they go the more they are conscious of the changing mix of faces. Then the style and neatness of the dress, shown up by the rivulets of like attire and aspect, which start to coalesce along pedestrian routes. Walking further beyond the centre, black faces predominate as the European town metamorphoses finally into the scattering of rusted iron and boarding which is the invariable signature of most native locations. But most visitors will not venture that far, although, from a vantage point, they might look over to Korsten, a settlement on its own, an 'independent state' some say because it lies outside the boundary of the city and its suburbs. It was not so far that it could not serve the function of accommodation for workers and families, but it was beyond the reach of the 1903 Act on property ownership and segregation, beyond the edict of the Health Inspector, beyond the grasp of many municipal and private landlords and their police enforcers. In the end it lost its independence, but that was not for a bit yet.

I had got into the habit of wandering around neighbourhoods, aimlessly, you might say, but then I'm in my fifties now. When I started as a reporter in my twenties, I needed an assignment, something to give me direction, but now it's different, it's more like following where the action beckons. I suppose you could call it the reporter's nose. And the new editor-in-chief eventually loosened up a bit on me. Not like back in the early twenties after the Baakens Street affair, back then I scared them a bit, the powers that be, they didn't want me to tell it how it was. Now I get some freedom, though for the wrong reason, unfortunately. The government has made progress – that's their word not mine – on segregation. And the municipality is gradually getting their own way – New Brighton, that's the flagship Location for blacks – is finally developing how they want and, like I said, they will take over Korsten in the end. So the tide is turning and now the newspaper feels more secure, enough to take the chance to re-discover a bit of integrity and offer some counter argument. And I'm the one getting pushed to the front.

So I wander. Like today. I scan the groups on walkways, in shops, hanging around at corners, sitting at the roadside, Black White Coloured Asian Afrikaaner Xhosa Mfengu British Dutch French German Khoisan... we're all colours of the rainbow. There is a crowd over there on the other side of the road, they've stopped under a brabejum tree, which is sprawling its umbrella-covering out from a small waste patch by the road; a couple of men are lounging on the ground propping their heads on their hands, a few men are crouched looking up at two animated debaters. Most of the group are men, but there are four or five women standing relaxed, their chins on one hand, elbows supported by the other arm, pelvis loosely flexed to one side, a common pose for looking on. They are Xhosa. I only understand a little Xhosa. The argument looks political but all have the same reactions, so I am interested in how much difference there is between the two contenders. I cross the road, I only have the small camera, but I catch the eye of one of the women who looks in my direction and I motion for permission to take a photograph. She looks alarmed, her eyes show it immediately, and she grabs the arm of the woman alongside her and gesticulates in my direction, the men now look over my way, but more impassive than aggressive, and the second woman starts to walk towards me, slowly, calmly, gracefully. Her presence was familiar. It was the mother of the bride at that wedding, the assignment I wasn't interested in, until the next day when I saw the photographs. And... before that... yes, now I remember… it was her… with a baby… that was it, East London… 20 years ago, no, more… "thank you Mr Neumann… this is my daughter Ngoxolo…" With Frank, the English Frank, that's it…

"You are Nobomi".

She showed no surprise. Just that look again. And she smiled.

"Please come and meet my friends."

It was the start of a new chapter.

~~~

You will already have an idea from what I have said, that politics in a community such as ours was complicated. I saw it as a kind of screen on which the image was constantly shifting and re-forming. So many significant groups, and these were not small minorities, the Indians, the Asians, the coloureds, the several Europeans, but the largest population in the Eastern Cape were black Africans, mainly Xhosa, like Nobomi and her friends. In their different ways, all somehow sometime found a voice, but that did not mean they were heard where it mattered. For the Africans, certainly, there were African newspapers, but the Establishment was white, and, despite a growing African middle class, the Eastern Province Herald, my employer, was an establishment (and therefore White-orientated) newspaper.

The men in the group were cautious – that would do for me, at least they were not hostile – but the women were nervous. Nobomi introduced me as the reporter at her daughter's wedding, that's all – did she remember me from East London I wondered? – and she thought I might listen to what they wanted for their community and how they wanted their village – Korsten – to have help to improve conditions, but not at the expense of losing out to control by the city.

"Would you help us by telling people what we want without having them think we are dangerous?"

"They think you are dangerous because they are afraid of the African unions," I replied, "and black people are a majority."

"We are not the unions, but unions give black people a voice. Do you think it is bad, what the unions want?"

"I am a reporter. What I think myself does not matter."

"But your words can be like your camera. What is in the photograph is what you choose to be there. Your report is what you choose to say. Please help us. We need a voice which doesn't make white people afraid. Not everything ought to be black or white."

I don't mind saying… no, I do mind saying, because I am a seasoned reporter… but I felt uneasy. I can't put my finger on it. Reporter's instinct? But not just that, because the reporter's instinct is the objective view, whatever it is you're reporting on, however bad, it's out there and you're just in it to tell the story and you don't get involved. And I wasn't involved. I just happened to have recognised this woman Nobomi, I had photographed her for a friend and I had caught that look of hers, but that's what photographers do, so why should I be uneasy, and anyway that was over 20 years ago. No, this uneasiness, it can't be that…

No, it was that. She was my ghost. That's Mr Crosby again at the Dispatch, he used to say that anyone who had been in our business more than a few years had a ghost, a person who had come off the page and would stay in your mind for ever. Nobomi was my ghost. She had come off the page, that was certain. And now she was wandering around my life. I was excited, and a little afraid.

"In one way, I am on both sides, Mr Neumann. You might not realise but my daughter, Ngoxolo, whose wedding you photographed, she is half English."

"I do know. Frank told me." Once again no reaction, just that enigmatic smile.

After a lengthy political discussion under the brabejum tree with the group of friends, Nobomi had brought me back to her home in Korsten. One of the men had come too, but it was clear that this was not because of any romantic attachment. Rather I had the impression he thought he was there for her protection. Not that Nobomi gave any hint of anxiety, she seemed completely at ease, so perhaps the concern was with Uuka – that was his name – and his friends.

"I would like to call you Adam, if that is alright."

"You remember my name?"

"Of course. You took a risk for us, for Ngoxolo and me and Frank... and Harry in a way, because he would have wanted his mother to see our child... and I had no-one else to go to... there was only Frank."

"Why did you leave?"

After a long pause... "I cried when I left... Frank, he was such a good man... honest, straightforward, honourable... a real English gentleman – (she smiled as she said this) – but I would have brought him down... this country would have brought him down."

For long moments she was lost in her thoughts, then...

"I would like you to be around, if that wouldn't be a burden for you. You see, Ngoxolo is my only connection with Harry, and you, you are my only connection with Frank. Please stay close."

"I will."

"If Frank could know about this, I believe he would thank you." Another pause. "But Frank is dead."

That jolted me. How could she know? And anyway, why should he be? He was about my own age. I felt a vague emptiness starting to spread through me and shivered. English Frank.

"How do you know?" She seemed to be looking far into the distance.

"I knew that Harry was dead."

It was a year later that I found out that Frank had died only days before this conversation with Nobomi. His obituary notice had appeared in the Bristol Evening Post a few days afterwards:

> Francis Cole, engineer, son of Richard Symons Cole late of 25 St Michaels Hill Bristol : 9th February 1930 aged 50. He leaves a wife and four children.

~~~

I wondered how this was going to work. As usual I had gone in feet first, reminiscent of my younger days, carried away by my emotions, yes, that was it, that was always how these things happened to me... I had said 'yes' to Frank when I had been a rookie and would have been sacked for borrowing the company's equipment for my own use, I had once 'lost' a story which would have put a young African mother in jail – took a photograph out of our archives that time as well just to make sure she couldn't be recognised, I had written that piece about the Baakens Street riot which was never going to get published – lucky too, because they'd have put *me* in jail for that… and here I was again, carried away by something about the presence of this woman, whose name meant 'mother of life' and looks at you in a way I had never encountered before, with a composure which seemed to say "this is just how it is, let it be".

"What do you mean when you say 'please stay close'?"

"Oh, I don't mean I want a partner or anything like that, please understand, I will never have another partner, there was only ever Harry and there will never be anyone else. But… maybe like Frank. An Austrian Frank. I wonder if that could be."

"I am Jewish also, not just Austrian."

"A Jewish Frank, then."

We sat silently, simply looking at each other. Somehow it was not uncomfortable. Then she said, "There are many things I would like to tell you, some are things which might be useful for your articles, but some are about us – about my daughter Ngoxolo and what she does, and her husband. They are things you must keep to yourself." She sighed, and looked down, seeming to be talking to herself as much as me, "Many years ago, when I was wandering the countryside on my own with Ngoxolo as a baby, I had a dream. We Xhosa believe in dreams, for medicine and for knowing our path, we believe dreams are the ancestors talking. I am waiting. I feel the message the dream brought is getting closer. And sometimes I am afraid."

At that moment Uuka, who had gone out into the yard once he was confident I presented no threat, came back in with some beers. It seemed a fitting way to bring the afternoon to a close. We sat on the floor the three of us – Nobomi and I were talking about trivial things, Uuka said nothing – and a little later I was able to politely depart.

I left the dilapidation of Korsten and walked back to the city and my own very different surroundings.

~~~

Things had settled down slowly after the Baakens Street calamity. I suppose it took almost 3 years, but eventually the old order seemed to re-assert itself. It had helped when Walter Rubusana, whom Masabalala had assaulted, indirectly sparking off Baakens Street, refused to prosecute and so Masabalala could be released and could pursue the minimum wage negotiations, eventually securing some concessions. This and the cost of living coming down because prices were falling again after the war all contributed to a lowering of tension. By 1930 it seemed as though there was a way for the worst grievances to be settled. But that was premature.

The rest of my report... that's funny, I hadn't been thinking of it like that, but I suppose it could be like one of those features they put in the smart newspapers – anyway, you need to set it in a context which is probably very difficult for you to imagine. This was the time in South Africa of more or less haphazard segregation (in its various forms) slowly moving towards apartheid as a unilateral policy. But during the next 15 years or so of transition, none of the boundaries were clear, there were compromises everywhere and vicious battles between organisations which should have been on the same side. It was the infancy of the ANC[4], though at that time they were the most conciliatory of the groups campaigning for dignity and just conditions; the ICU[5] and the IWA[6] as sparring partners; the growing Communist Party of South Africa[7]... all this and more, the upshot of 250 years of reluctant (by some) and resistant (by others) and willing (yet others) assimilation by native peoples into an alien culture and economic system. For the black majority the pressures, in the end, were too great to resist – the British force of arms, the privations of destitution, the humility of discrimination – and then the wrecker in the ranks, the

---

[4] The African National Congress (originally the South African Native National Congress) was founded in 1912 and for almost 30 years was led by lawyers, clergy and journalists, sought white support and used constitutional processes.

[5] The Industrial and Commercial Workers Union was formed amongst dock-workers in Cape Town in 1919, but in the end drew most of its support from the countryside and tenant landowners.

[6] The Industrial Workers of Africa dissolved in 1921.

[7] The Communist Party of South Africa was constituted in 1922 following the disbanding of the IWA.

basic human urge for kudos, which corrupts public action and private interaction alike with that ever-present and imponderable question hanging over all our best intentions – what sacrifice is justified for how much gain? – the impossible dilemma between the one and the many.

I saw Nobomi every few weeks, almost always at her house in Korsten. To call it a house is generous, though to describe it as a shack, which is what it really was, feels patronising. It was her home. Four tin walls on a wooden frame with a partition which divided the sleeping space – little bigger than the bed itself – from the rest. The standard brasier fire with a stove-pipe chimney in the centre between the cooking and the sitting space. The sitting space covered with boards had a chair and some cushions on the floor, and we generally sat on the floor. The cooking area had an earth floor and a sink on a stand, which served for any activity needing water, the water having to be carried from a standpipe two lots down the road. All the cooking happened on the brasier in the middle, which was permanently alight. The toilet was in a roofless wooden cubicle about four feet square in a corner of the yard, from which water and excrement washed down a channel under the wall and into a soak-away. Korsten was notorious for its insanitary conditions – most people in the city called it a slum – and the State Health Inspector was always looking for ways to enforce regulations to condemn the houses and move out the inhabitants to the New Brighton location with a view to demolishing the whole place. It did not come under the control of the municipality and much official time had been spent on looking for legal ways to extend this jurisdiction, but it would have required approval from the government in Cape Town. Then to enact a demolition would still need co-ordination between state agencies and local management. In addition, the inhabitants of the village had a spirit of independence and a little economic influence, for their labour was needed in the city and their ease of access was an advantage to many employers. So Korsten survived for a few more years, desultory and dilapidated on its barren hillock.

Inside number 56 you could have found us, Nobomi and me, usually with others of her friends, sitting on the cushions on the floor, the pan simmering constantly on the brasier for the next round of coffees or tea – beer was the exception – talking in the semi-darkness, sometimes quietly, attentively, listening to one another, waiting to offer a response, sometimes giving way to excitement, sometimes noisily proclaiming a new idea, then oblivious to the rest until finally halted, usually by a quiet intervention. Yes, that would always be Nobomi: if you were sitting with our group, it would not have taken you long to notice that the one whose presence could be felt most strongly was the one who said the least and watched the most.

I was beginning to see these groups as models for academic seminars – the discussions could be vigorous but always in the end there was an agreement that different paths could co-exist and so long as some development was happening then it could be trusted that improved conditions would result. I wondered sometimes whether the whole thing might not have been a performance for my benefit to show this stooge of the white establishment that the African, even the lower class manual minimum-wage African, was buying into the politico-economic system of the minority (white) governing elite and their platform of a multi-ethnic 'liberal' society rewarded on merit. That might sound like the wishful thinking of the writer of an election manifesto, but you must remember that an African bourgeoisie was now well established and striving (in vain) for parity with their white peers. Unfortunately, they had bought into an economic system which was working to ensure that intellectual and professional equivalence would never mean financial equality. To compound the anomaly, the liberal African, mission-school educated, smart western-dressed, perceived no racial distinction with a white colleague, but might feel a clear divide when he met a black compatriot who was working class and a manual labourer.

We were a few sessions on before my impression of our meetings at number 56 changed, and then it came from an unexpected quarter.

It was the first time that Ngoxolo, Nobomi's daughter had come to one of our afternoons, that is to say, one at which I had been present. She sat away from her mother and perhaps it was this that emphasised the differences between them. Where Nobomi gently gazed, Ngoxolo seemed to scrutinise; where Nobomi received a speaker's words like the touch of a friend, Ngoxolo seemed to hold them at a distance in case they challenged; where Nobomi spoke as if to meet the speaker, Ngoxolo seemed to counter and compete. I was surprised to be making such comparisons, thinking that what I would have noticed first would have been that she was not pure Xhosa, but those differences, of which only two come to mind, were secondary. I was puzzled that what I recalled most distinctly about her father Harry that Frank had told me, was almost the opposite of what I saw in her. And the opposite of how I saw her mother also. Harry had been easy-going, Frank had said, enquiring and accepting of whatever came, a gentle presence in the world. But the only trace of him in his daughter that was visible to me was her hair, which was not curly black like her mother's, but more wavy and a slightly auburn dark brown. I was puzzled and I wondered if my observations could be connected with Nobomi's request that I "please stay close". Ngoxolo seemed not to be surprised by my presence and, when told that I was from the Herald, but unofficially, by one of the men, had remarked that she hoped I had come to educate myself and not as a means of furthering the illusion of black/white equality in social ranking.

That meeting was around the time Korsten residents were starting to become anxious about their future. Pressure was increasing now that the village was incorporated within the city boundary. The Medical Officer of Health was quick to take advantage and had started inspections with a view to clearing most of the habitations and forcing Africans to move to the Municipality's New Brighton location to make way for demolitions. About half of our 'regulars' lived in Korsten, the rest either in the city as exempted Africans, as did Ngoxolo and her husband, or illegally. That much I knew and I also knew, because Nobomi had mentioned it, that Ngoxolo's husband was an official in the Port Elizabeth branch of the ANC. But the more I listened to Ngoxolo and built up a picture of her ideas and opinions, the more it surprised me that she could be the wife of an ANC official, given the ANC at that time were still working through representation and petitions and the various consultative councils to improve the pay and living conditions of Africans. They were still a long way removed from the militancy which was growing in the ICU and spilling over into the attitudes of many ordinary working folk in the locations, such as Korsten and New Brighton.

My attendance at the meetings, which were generally weekly, became regular. You would probably have said that I was being a little naïve in thinking that such regularity would not be noticed or, if it was, would not be a matter of some interest in a city of around 80,000 people. Over the years I had met and spoken to a very large number of people and I suppose my face would be recognised more than most, but it came like a bolt from the blue when, alone with Nobomi after one of the meetings, she said to me that I should take different routes coming to the meetings and try not to attract attention. I thought at first that she was concerned that my (obviously) non-African appearance should not create difficulties for other members, but it was not that. She was concerned for me. And not as a White exposed amongst Africans, but as a White amongst fellow Whites. She didn't expand, but she said that sometimes she got this 'sense of things' without being able to tell why. Intuition? I suggested. But she said that it was more physical and seemed to be a response to an atmosphere.

That was the first shadow.

The second came a few days later with a phone call to my office from the Magistrate's clerk saying that the Magistrate would like to have my views and feedback on the recent public meeting on the re-alignment of city sectors for exempted Africans. This was a contentious subject and despite the meeting having been promulgated as an exercise in open consultation, because of a last-minute change of venue and time, it was in reality the opposite. I would not normally have thought any more about it, even though it was not a request I would have expected, had it not been for Nobomi's concern that I be wary about who may be noticing my movements.

My suspicion was justified, because the invitation to give my views and feedback was in fact a manoeuvre to subject me to a condemnation of my style of reporting and in particular my questioning (in my article on the 'public' consultation) of the motive for re-timing and re-locating a meeting that had long been publicised for public attendance.

After these two incidents, though, everything went quiet. I did not even get summoned by the Herald's bosses, who would for certain have known of my interview by the Magistrate. It did mean, however, that I asked myself some questions about what I believed in and where I was going, the usual man's midlife stuff, except that I was fast getting beyond midlife. The romantic question came up as well, of course. I had got used to a bachelor's existence, which does have advantages for a reporter, but that did not mean I wanted to consign myself to a solitary old age. (I should have mentioned that my wife had died many years before and we had never had children.) If I'm honest, it was no coincidence that such thoughts would come up around this same time. I had come to feel myself a genuine affiliate of the group (which had taken to calling itself Korsten Action or KA for short) and had often found myself alone with Nobomi, invariably talking about politics or philosophy and sharing a beer after a meeting. It appeared she had concerns for my safety – alright that is a natural human thing – but then hadn't she said back in the early days "Please stay close". Not a Harry, but a Frank. I was too old to be a Harry any more, but Frank? I remembered that I really liked Frank. But Frank is dead. And Nobomi knew before I told her. How was that possible?

You can hear how this woman was starting to fascinate me... she seemed to challenge and inspire. And without seeking or claiming it, she attracted loyalty – Uuka certainly... and now me.

~~~

But my worries were not over. I say "my worries", though I was increasingly thinking of them as "our worries". Nobomi was the principal addition that 'our' was encompassing, but not far beyond was Ngoxolo who by then was 7 months pregnant. All the things that happened to us over the next years came from the Municipality's change of boundaries and determination to clear out Korsten on the pretext that it was a slum, which indeed large parts of it were. But you might also suspect pride as a motivation because Korsten had succeeded in maintaining its status as a 'free state' against the tide of complete social segregation, which was steadily advancing across South Africa. From 1931, when the Municipality obtained legal jurisdiction, until the start of the Second World War War in 1939 there were successive and progressive attempts to take over and flatten large parts of the location. By the time the Municipality finally succeeded they had inflicted more than a decade of strife and corruption on its struggling residents. Until my involvement with Nobomi's group I could take the observer stance of a reporter, albeit a liberal observer with a conscience, but something inside me had shifted in the last few months: no longer the outsider, I was invested in the cause. It had become part of me.

I believe now that the next incident, or rather my involvement, was set up as a test of my loyalty to the establishment, that is the Municipality and its policies and agents, with the Herald as one of those. In exercise of their powers under the 1930 Slum Act, the Municipality were repeatedly carrying out inspections in Korsten, condemning a few properties and forcibly removing their residents to houses in New Brighton which was to the north and further from the city itself. Usually these 'raids' (for that is really what they were) by Health Department officials were carried out during daylight hours and the targets were mostly men living in multiple occupancy single-room shacks. On this occasion, though, the raid was after dark and accompanied by police and an Assistant Magistrate. Also, three families were targeted. All were evicted and, when a substantial crowd of onlookers started to form, more police were sent for. I had just left Nobomi's house and heard the commotion starting in the distance – was it already known, which day I usually spent the afternoon in Korsten? – and I made my way towards the noise which was coming from the 'Village', the central and slightly more reputable part of the location. Two families were being moved, the usual anonymous vans standing outside two adjacent two-room houses. To my dismay, one of these was the home of one of our members. Claiming press privilege I managed to gain entry to this one and almost get close enough to confront the Assistant Magistrate before being forcibly ejected by two police. I tried at the back to get close enough to see what was happening inside, only to be threatened with arrest. At this point, realising there was just a possibility of filing a story in the next two hours which could be included in the following day's edition, I took the shortest route back to the Herald's offices and set to work. The following brief account made the first edition:

> Your reporter fortuitously arrived this evening on the scene of an unfortunate action forcibly prosecuted against innocent members of our populace. Departing from established procedure officials from the Department of Health, accompanied by police and under cover of darkness, visited three homes in Korsten for inspection of sanitary practices and standards and evicted two families with children. Despite his legitimate claim to press privileges this reporter was removed before he was able to interview on your behalf, good readers, the Assistant Magistrate, who was also present. He was unable to obtain identities or justification for the action, being threatened himself with arrest. It is to be hoped that the Magistrate's Office will act promptly to clarify the reason, if any, for this departure from procedure and protocol without notice.

The story only made the first edition and first printing before being discovered and removed by our management. By the time I learnt this shortly after my arrival the following morning, though, there was something of far greater concern about to break. From a junior colleague I heard that a woman had been arrested at 56 Korsten and was being held by police in connection with one of the families who had been evicted. It could only be Nobomi.

Before I had a chance to leave the building I was caught by the Senior Director demanding that I accompany him to the boardroom. Already seated down one side of the directors' table were two other directors of the newspaper and the Magistrate himself. Although for a moment I thought this was convenient because it would save me a journey and a long wait for a meeting, it was the first worrying indication that I might have been set up for this the previous evening and even that my movements were somehow being monitored.

The meeting, no, my interrogation, began in the anodine way you would probably expect, with almost casual requests for information and clarification – had I received a tipoff that there was going to be a story at Korsten? – did I have an intelligence source in the Department of Health? – was there a reason for my being in Korsten at that hour? – what made me consider these particular evictions worthy of a story, when such inspections were happening justifiably and quite frequently? – what justification did I have for bypassing normal editorial procedure and obliging the typesetters to insert my copy at such an hour? This last question was the one they really wanted the answer to, of course, and the answer was that there were others in the newspaper who had similar sympathies to my own and I knew who I could trust. I need hardly tell you that this was the question to which they got the least helpful answer.

I received token plaudits for my concern to present information to our readers in as timely a manner as possible and using my own free time in pursuing the newspaper's business. These were delivered by the Senior Director in an expressionless monotone while the others seated opposite me simply looked on with no outward sign of interest at all. But the tone became harsh and uncompromising when he started on his string of criticisms, which included unreasonable demands to staff to flout regulations, failure to notify management of my activities at the earliest possible opportunity, biased and possibly false reporting of events, failure to uphold the Herald's standards of editorial neutrality, inappropriate political comment… the list went on. And now the onlookers were far from disinterested with approving nods and words of affirmation echoing the Senior Director's catalogue of 'misdemeanours'. My punishment? I was forbidden to write or contribute to any story with political content or with subject matter which was "contentious for our body politic".

My decision required little reflection. By the end of the afternoon I had given my letter of resignation to the Senior Director's secretary and done the rounds of like-minded colleagues from delivery-hands to editors explaining that I had not been sacked but gagged and I was not prepared to compromise my professional integrity.

I walked away from my life's work with some apprehension. I thought of my dear wife, so long gone.

~~~

Nobomi had been arrested on suspicion of making skokiaan and hosting illegal drink parties. Now I know Nobomi always had some beer around for the occasional drink if our meetings went on later into the evening, but you could not mistake her for a skokiaan queen. Free now to act as a private individual, I went straight round to Baakens Street and remonstrated with the most senior police officer I could find. To no avail. It came to the point that I was threatened with arrest for sheltering non-exempted Africans who were contravening Pass Law regulations in my own house, it being within the city and off limits to such. I left dejected and depressed that it was now possible for an official to spout any lie which might come to mind in order to deflect inconvenient enquiries.

Nobomi was released after 48 hours without explanation and returned to find her home had been ransacked in her absence, perhaps to find evidence to support the fabricated allegation, but more likely to find records of the people who regularly gathered there, though there were none.

Or perhaps it was pure spite.

Once more the feeling of threat, which I felt around me like a periodic shadow cast by the sun as it passes behind clouds, once more, it eased. But, as when clouds become more frequent and the bright intervals shorter until finally the whole sky is covered and darkens with the approach of a storm, so the disturbances became more frequent and discontent more evident in the demeanour of people in their everyday lives... fewer greetings, sullen avoidant faces, more frequent confrontations, a tenseness around the city, locations and townships alike. Amongst the members of Korsten Action a greater caution, about meetings – rarely outside now, even in the bright summer weather – and in the conduct of their day-to-day activities, a wariness in their contact with strangers.

On 24th July 1934 another Nobomi was born. It seems strange to say it like that, as if it were some sort of reincarnation, but we all knew she would be called Nobomi, for a long time before she was born. And if the baby had been a boy? Well, all I can say is that the possibility never came into question.

About a year later Nobomi was again arrested. Since the birth of little Nobomi she had been accustomed to spending more time at the house of Ngoxolo and Themba in the city, to look after the baby. On occasions she would stay overnight if Ngoxolo was accompanying Themba to a meeting or an event and they did not arrive back until later in the evening. Unlike her daughter and husband, Nobomi was non-exempted. Despite being a professional, educated and middle-class African, Themba had been unable to obtain exempted status for his mother-in-law, which would have allowed her to stay in the city beyond the limits that her Pass dictated. Staying overnight, even with her own daughter's family was an infringement. It was certain that sooner or later she would be reported, such was the level of suspicion and distrust that was building up within communities and the inevitable incentive for betrayal to gain official favour for advantage. Was it a neighbour or was it an ANC colleague who knew that the couple would not have left their daughter with just anyone, that it would be certain to be Ngoxolo's mother? The police arrived at midnight and Nobomi was taken once more to Baakens Street. Once more they held her much longer than was customary for a first Pass Law offence. Once more I visited the magistrate's office seeking to use my fast dwindling credibility as a widely-respected member of the community to secure her release. Again to no avail. They released her when they wanted to. This time she spent 3 nights in custody.

I reflected on how easily we allow ourselves to become accustomed to circumstances in our lives which are imposed on us and are recurrent. It seems to be a battle between conserving the energy needed to survive and feeding our spirit with the hope of change by railing at the injustices. And the ever-present risk of complacency creeping in – accepting the status quo because it is always easier to deal with what you know.

So it was with us for the next 3 years or so: I eked out enough of a living by writing for journals and designing leaflets and prospectuses; little Nobomi spent more and more time with her grandmother to make it possible for her mother to take a teaching position in the best-regarded school for Africans; Themba became known as one of the most trustworthy accountants in the city as well as progressing in the ranks of the ANC.

It was now 1938.

Korsten Action had lost several of its members as a result of the Municipality's increasingly forceful attempts to clear all African residents. With one exception they had chosen, once their houses had been demolished to rejoin their families in the country. Two others had given way to the authority's pressure and voluntarily moved to New Brighton having been persuaded by the latest offer of free travel from there to the Port where they worked and three-room houses for their families at the same rent as their one-room shacks in Korsten. Always as much involved in activities to improve the living environment as in campaigns to fight for better wages and more employment, we were trying to re-invent ourselves with the identity of a peaceful pressure group and promote our argument through constant visibility. We developed slogans and organised weekly gatherings on roads at the main entry points on the city's boundary. Alongside this, there was a welfare support and action group which offered educational activities, as well as advocacy work on behalf of families who were in dispute with the authorities, whether this was the Health Department, the Municipality, the police or their own employer. As with many a new departure, initial growth was fast, spurred on by a handful of imaginative slogans and one or two very visible and successful marches. With a motto of Peaceful Persistence we were able to achieve a few small but visible successes in the first months. Then came the problems of holding together what was growing to become a loose collection of personal interests and differing views in an environment inured to force and double-cross as normal means of pursuing private goals.

Little Nobomi came almost daily now to be cared for by her grandmother and, since the harassment of her grandmother by the police (who had determined that caring for a child, other than as official employment in the city, was an infringement of the Pass Law in her case) increased to the point where there appeared to be a police officer posted strategically to intercept her on her way to collect her charge, I had taken on the roll of accompanying the child from her parents' house to Nobomi's at 56 Korsten. Fortunately I was managing to make enough of a living to retain my car, or the problem for all of us would have been much greater. So, from editor-reporter to child chauffeur... and to be honest I took quite a delight in it.

Occasionally I collected her again from Korsten and took her home, which meant that I was able to have conversations with Ngoxolo and sometimes with Themba as well. It wasn't difficult to imagine Ngoxolo as a teacher, for she was clear and analytic in her manner. I wondered whether some would find her too pedagogic, though I did not think this was her intention in any overbearing way, but rather that it came from her wish to ensure that she had expressed herself unambiguously. By contrast, Themba had more the presence and aura of her mother by whom more was conveyed non-verbally, and whose openness, shown by her attentive listening, allowed the speaker to see themselves, as it were, in a mirror and come to a resolution in which they truly believed.

But that evening Ngoxolo was quieter, almost hesitant, as she began: "I trust you, Adam. More than anyone in KA, even though they are my own people. I know you will say – what has 'own people' got to do with it – but I grew up in Korsten, remember, and even though Nobomi was my mother, we two are different. I have never had a Harry or a Frank. I'm rambling, aren't I, and that's not like me. My Themba could be under threat from so many quarters. Maybe I am a threat too. He is a liberal and a moderate. He wants change too and in his own way is fighting for it. He says that all people in South Africa must be able to be who they are, he calls it non-racialism, and that we should trust co-operation and collaboration, because we all have the same human nature, Black White Coloured Indian, in the end we will all be together as one community. If we are patient, he says. I believe that as well, but not the patient bit. I am afraid his way will take too long."

"Then are you worried about you and him?"

"No. Not that. In the end we will walk a path together. And now, with little Nobomi... No, we each want the other one to be themselves, then we can each be ourselves. It works. For us. But there are others, who are not patient like him and they believe they can have their way over him."

"These others don't believe in co-operation and collaboration."

"No."

"And sometimes you are threatened?"

"Often, now. There are so many people who want to make this part of the world as *they* say it *should* be. More and more in the ANC say that the party's old way of collaboration that Themba believes in should be changed. Some look at the Communist Party and the African Unions and want to be like them. But there is often violence in their methods. Some want to expel all Whites from the ANC, but surely then we break communication? – Themba believes that is never a good thing. Some even think they can do a deal with the disgruntled landlords to get them into power on the Council. They think that will get them influence and then they will take over."

"What do you believe?"

Ngoxolo took her time, then: "I believe there will not be peace in South Africa until the Whites are not afraid of us. But those who think there would be peace if there were no more Whites are wrong. Difference makes conflict. That is true. But there will always be difference… Xhosa, Zulu, Mfengu, Khoisan, Sotho… Black and White is just the difference you notice first."

I thought to myself how I would feel privileged to be one of Ngoxolo's pupils.

"But I am worried now more than before," she pulled herself back to immediate things, "because Themba had a message from one of his group of supporters for re-election in the ANC saying they wanted a meeting about his policies because they wanted him to be more hardline. That's where he is tonight."

She went on: "It's worse than that. I was called in by our Principal and told that I must be careful how I express myself because if it was interpreted that I was saying that segregation was immoral because it was against human nature and human rights, then the school could lose the support of the Municipality. He went on and said, 'We cannot say that segregation is always wrong, because it was the Europeans who first built our towns and the Africans who wanted to leave the land and work in towns, but the two have different cultures and not everything can be mixed.' Can you believe that? Our Principal is Xhosa and a Christian."

She paused for breath. "It feels like they are closing in on us from both sides."

"Who are the more dangerous 'they'?"

"I would like to know." And then, "Please take good care of Nobomi."

For one short moment, it felt as if there was only one Nobomi. "I will. I promise."

I would not have long to wait for my promise to be tested.

At that moment Themba arrived back. He looked harrassed. I excused myself and left.

The following day I was not surprised to find him waiting at my house on my return from delivering Nobomi to her grandmother.

"Thank you, Adam, for helping us as you do with little Nobomi. I know that Ngoxolo mentioned some of our worries to you last night, but I am here to tell you things that she will not have known then. I have to tell you that you also might be in danger because many people know of your connections with us and with Ngoxolo's mother and KA."

We were drinking tea in my kitchen and Themba had the almost furtive air of a man unsure from where the next attack might come. "The Municipality wants to destroy

KA because they believe it has been taken over by communist worker gangs. They blame you because of your articles in the Herald. They know you are a member. You should not go there. Now you have enemies in the city and in Korsten."

"I have made a promise."

"I will try again to get a Pass for Nobomi to come into the city. But I do not think they will do it for me."

After Themba had left I remembered Frank's solution. Around 30 years ago he had 'employed' Nobomi as his housemaid after Harry died. She had no-one else and it was the only way to keep her with him as segregation got more rigid in East London. As well, Ngoxolo had been born and Nobomi was depressed. But later she left him and disappeared. I was pondering on how she had left when there was nowhere else for her to go, and her words from one of the early afternoons in 56 Korsten came to mind again – "… like Frank, an Austrian Frank." Would she come here? I dismissed the notion – today's Nobomi was not the bereaved and vulnerable young mother. But she had said, "Please stay close." I was hoping I could stay close enough.

That afternoon I went across to Korsten earlier than usual to collect little Nobomi. I excused my uninvited early arrival, though there was no need and I was invited to sit and take some tea. As I arrived I had noticed Uuka standing on the corner opposite and I remarked on this. "He is there or around all of the day," she said, "sometimes he does a job for me, sometimes I have in him for tea, sometimes he stands with friends who are talking there, sometimes he plays cricket with boys in the street," she smiled, "he can only play wicket, he is too big for anything else. But everyone knows he will never be far away from me. And no-one will try to fight Uuka."

"No need for an Austrian Frank," I said.

"Not yet, Adam, but I am afraid. The time for Austrian Frank is coming soon." She sounded oddly certain, which gave her remark a chillingly prophetic feel.

It was getting dark, the sky was heavy, I felt more anxious than usual to have little Nobomi in her own home – Korsten was a darkly desolate place when the light was gone. As we left I looked across at Uuka, still standing with two others, and we exchanged complicit nods.

~~~

When the end came it was swift. One of the scenes had already been played, though I did not know this until many years later when an old colleague on the Herald tracked me down and wrote to me.

Themba had a distant cousin, Bhutana, who was the second son of the Principal at the school where Ngoxolo taught. He was also in the ANC and, strongly influenced by his father and so was a believer in the traditional collaborative philosophy of the Party. 'Participation not Protest' was his slogan, the product of a Black middle-class professional family who had an interest in moving along a course to ever greater social acceptance in the white man's sphere. One evening he had found his father troubled in a way he had not previously seen him. Earlier that day his father had dismissed Ngoxolo after a complaint and threats from an influential parent who was a member of the Municipal Council. She had told his son's class about the ANC and the ICU, which had given way to the Communist party, and how they were following different roads and the question for all Africans was not just which road they were going to take, but also how long it was going to take. Ngoxolo was summoned and had been involved in a fierce disagreement with the Principal – he thought he remembered her accusing him of betraying his principals, no longer being the honest educator – and he had told her to leave and not to return. Bhutana saw his father's distress and felt his own anger rising – over the years he had used doctors to try to handle it but with little result – and he saw the hurt in his father's face such as he had never seen before. Then a different anger, of a more insidious kind, at the prospect of his own life-course of growing wealth and influence being thwarted – fuel on the fire.

So part of the final scene had been set.

~~~

In the early morning of the last day, a police contingent with a plain black detention van arrived outside the house of Themba and Ngoxolo. They arrested Themba on suspicion of sedition and took him to Baakens Street. In one of those strange quirks of fate which we usually allow to pass unremarked, little Nobomi had not come back with me from 56 Korsten the day before, when I arrived to take her home, but had stayed the night with her grandmother. It was the first (and only) time this happened. I could not tell whose idea it had been, but both had seemed very excited about it. As I left, Nobomi had said to me, "Tell Ngoxolo she has to stay with me tonight, Adam."

When the police had driven Themba away and forbidden Ngoxolo to follow him, six officers remained who proceeded to ransack the house. They made her stand, shaking uncontrollably, in the middle of the main room as they looked in every corner, turned out every drawer, cleared every cupboard, slashed open every chair, tore apart every mattress and, finding nothing which interested them, left two hours later. Ngoxolo waited half an hour and then came to my house. I didn't live far away, but she took a long route in order to avoid being followed. It was 10 when she arrived. I considered going straight to Baakens Street despite her protests, but then thought better and phoned one of my former colleagues at the Herald. The story hadn't landed and he was pleased to be first in with it. He would contact the Magistrate's office immediately and phone me back. We waited. For more than two hours we waited.

It was into the afternoon when another former colleague arrived at my house. He explained that he had come because the first call to the Magistrate's office had unleashed a string of callbacks to the Senior Director. Martin had been afraid to make a call out or leave the office himself for fear of giving away his source. The only information the police would give was that a close relative of Themba, who was also a member of the ANC, had uncovered incitement to violent protest in Themba's papers, intended to challenge the Municipal Council. Themba would be interrogated over the next 48 hours and would appear before the Magistrate after that. In the meantime, the police had been ordered to find and arrest Ngoxolo.

I sent the reporter away before talking to Ngoxolo. She was desperate to see her daughter and of course there were only two possible locations, here at my house or at 56 Korsten. Assuming that now we were trying to keep four of us together, Korsten seemed the better choice – fewer infringements by travelling, plus Uuka as a bodyguard and hopefully other friends close by.

In the gathering dusk of the last day, we set off in my car for 56 Korsten. Ngoxolo was sitting directly behind the driver's seat with the curtains drawn across the side windows. I avoided Main Street so as not to go directly through the city. We took a little under half an hour. In Korsten I left the road and parked the car on a side track behind a brabejum tree, which would conceal it once darkness had fallen. It left us 200 yards to walk to number 56. It was very quiet for early in the evening, I thought, the distant clangour usually carried on the wind seeming hushed and the roadway deserted – no occasional passerby, no friends talking on a corner, no neighbours sitting out. No Uuka. I felt my stomach churn. Where was the watchful giant? We arrived at 56. Nobomi heard us and opened the door the instant we were there and shut it quickly after us. She slid the bolt and fastened the padlock. I wondered whether the soundness of the door frame matched the weight of bar and padlock attached to it.

The brasier in the centre of the room was giving out good heat and there was a warm glow from its red embers. Never having been a father so always looking in, it has surprised me how children, particularly very young children can take themselves away into a world within a world and not reflect the anxiety of adults around. Even if they make an occasional foray into the adult zone with a picture or a question, still they can return to their own, unconcerned. So it was with little Nobomi playing on the floor with models her grandmother had made, while we exchanged what news we had. Nobomi was concerned, as I was, about the absence of Uuka, who had been asked by another member of KA to help with a heavy loading job on the other side of Korsten. It was only a few minutes away and would have taken less than half an hour. But that was 2 hours ago, before this eerie quiet had descended onto the location – yes, Nobomi had noticed the quiet too.

There was some vegetable stew bubbling and we sat around in silence forcing ourselves to eat something in case it would be a while before the opportunity came again. As we finished, lights passed across the window, white light diluting the warm glow, then extinguished. A vehicle had stopped somewhere on the road. Impossible to see out, the night was black. Two minutes, perhaps three, then a door, no, more than one. Several feet on the dirt road and a sense of slow advance towards our door.

Now came the heavy knock, just once, then twice.

A voice, not rough, more educated, but slurred by alcohol and shouting, "I want to speak to Ngoxolo."

Ngoxolo stood up – I reached for her in case she was going to go too close to the door, but no, she just stood a little way behind it and drew her breath in slowly – "What do you want?"

"You've corrupted your husband and betrayed his family."

"I've corrupted no-one."

"Themba believes your lies. They've taken him away when we needed him most. But it's you. Boomslang[8]. You are

---

[8] Highly venomous tree snake

poison. Now the police are coming for you. But I am here first."

"Who are you?"

"I am your husband's cousin. Open the door. You must pay to your family."

"If I have committed a crime I will be tried by a court."

There was silence, a faint sense of movement away from the door. Then breathing, becoming heavier. Now the ear-splitting yell of voices as 4 men charged the door with a tree trunk as battering ram, the sickening thud and splintering as the door-frame was ripped from the wall, a pounding of heavy feet invading desecrating violating...

Ngoxolo behind the door, now on the floor, I saw Bhutana kneeling over her, arm raised, he had a miner's pick-hammer and was striking down where her head must have been...

I leapt to protect little Nobomi, shield her, cover her eyes, but too late, her hands were by her face, her tiny nails digging into her cheeks and a scream like I had never heard before, "Noooooooooo............

Was it seconds or minutes?

Silence came slowly, spreading its blanket over eight mortals, one a child, one dead.

Then, gradually, a different kind of hush. A waiting. No, it was not over yet. Quick footsteps. Uuka, panting, was filling the space where the door had been. No-one moved. The time it takes the book to close. Bhutana knows. A thunderous roar, the hammer wrenched away, he knows, before the instant of the first excruciating crack, he knows, then still more… again, again, again… finally no more…

I had in the end managed to cover little Nobomi's eyes. Bhutana's companions had fled. Uuka now sitting drained against a wall, the blood-soaked hammer on the floor beside him.

Silence came again.

Six mortals now, one a child, two dead… finally no more.

I was holding Ngoxolo's child, her face buried against my chest.

Nobomi would be the next to speak.

We needed time to collect some shattered fragments from our ruptured lives, but now, now we had no time.

"I will tell you what has to happen. Then we will part, because the police will be coming. Uuka, it is very important for me that my Ngoxolo is laid to rest in a decent way and with her father. He is in East London Eastbank Cemetery. His grave is 590 in 5C. Please do this last thing for me, please take her there and bury her, and whatever you hear about me after this, do not come back here. I thank you from my heart for all your care for me."

Then she added, "Perhaps her daughter will come back one day to her."

"Adam, there will be no-one to care for little Nobomi and they will be looking for her as well. I will be gone for a long time. Will you take her away, as far away as you can from this place, from this country? When she is old enough she can decide if she wants to come back. When she is old enough please tell her about us, all of us. I thank you too from my heart for all you have done, for all you will do."

"Now you must go."

She stood and brought a covering from the bed and Uuka wrapped the body of Ngoxolo, gently hoisted her onto his shoulder and left.

I lifted little Nobomi who kept her head against me. I turned so that her grandmother could touch her face one last time. She had taken off the gold locket which she always wore, but never showed to anyone, and handed it to me, saying, "This is little Nobomi's now, please give it to her when she is a few years older. It comes from her English great great grandmother." I secreted it in an inside pocket and then I also left the unspeakable devastation.

Nobomi stayed, sitting alone with the murderer of the daughter who was her last connection to her beloved Harry.

We were safely in my car, hidden behind the brabejum tree when I heard the police arrive. When I was sure that all activity had finally ceased I drove to the house of a friend near the Port. I knew he could arrange a steamer passage. We would leave East London two days later bound for Madeira. There we would transfer lines and route to Trieste. From Trieste it would be an easy journey to my native Vienna.

The last day had ended.

part three

letter from Nobomi to John…

1st June 1954

Dear John

We did not come to harm. We are safe. I feel like like grandmother Nobomi, who told me that when she left her family home it was early one morning when everyone was asleep, because if she had told them they would have tried to stop her. But her father knew, she said. He knew she would be a wanderer and he used to say to her – ewe hamba, uyazulazula ndiyaqonda – it means, 'yes walk, wanderer, I understand'. I think you knew too, John. And I hope you too understand.

You will not be able to guess what has happened since you last saw us, so I will tell you. You will want to know because it is part of how I came to be in Vienna. You remember I could not tell you when you asked me. It was because I did not know. Well now I do, that is, I mostly know, because he would not tell me everything, as he thought it would be too painful. He is a man called Adam. He said he knew my mother and my grandmother when he lived in a place called Port Elizabeth in South Africa and one day my grandmother had asked him to take me away from there because bad things were happening and they would not be able to look after me any longer. My grandmother gave him her locket and told him to give it to me when I was older so that I knew he was a friend. I wanted to know what happened to my mother, but he said he could not tell me. So he brought me to Vienna because his family home was here. While the war was going on some Nazis came to the house where I was living too and stole what was valuable and destroyed the house and killed his old mother and father, and I must have thought they had killed him as well and I had to run away again. I lived with the children who were homeless in the city until Hugh found me. But Adam wasn't killed and when the war ended and Germany had to pay back what the Nazis had stolen from his people, he started his father's silver business again and made good money. Then one day he recognised me in the park when I was walking with Hugh. He wanted to be my benefactor, so he has put us on our way to Matatiele. Yes, Matatiele. Maybe, my grandmother too. Adam's people help each other and he arranged for us to go to London and then another place in England to get on a boat to South Africa. That is where we are now. We are getting on the boat today and we will arrive in a place called Port Elizabeth in two weeks.

John, I am happy and I am sad and I am worried, all mixed together. South Africa is not a happy place. I am black, but I do not look completely African, and Hugh is white. But Adam has contacted his community in Port Elizabeth and he says they will meet us and look after us and help us to go on to Matatiele.

You remember the evenings when we sat the three of us and looked out over the city in the room at the top? It looked as if there was a line at the end of the world where the sky started. But there isn't really, because as you move towards it, it goes further away. Does that mean that if we keep walking, one day we could find everyone we know again? If it does, I hope I find you again.

ndiyakuthanda, Nobomi

letter from Nobomi to John…

15th September 1954

Dear John

I am really sorry that I must write to you again. I have to ask for your help again because it has not gone well for Hugh these last weeks and I am not sure what I can do for him any longer. I think perhaps you will be able to tell me what to do. I hope that is possible.

I had great hope as we were on the way on the steamer, I could see how his spirit was becoming lighter. Each day I could see the tension in his face get less and he was able to talk more and he even began to talk to the people at our table in the saloon, who were complete strangers. That was new and I was so pleased for him. We also found some maps and we were starting to see how we could go from Port Elizabeth, perhaps find Harry's grave in East London, and get to Matatiele. I don't think that he had one of his night panics at all while we were on the steamer.

Since we arrived we have stayed with a man and his wife that Adam had arranged. They are older than us and they are Jewish – Adam had explained that this was how he had been able to make arrangements, because it meant he could find people he could trust. We have to be careful here because of the new regulations and the segregation and something called Pass Laws which are coming in. It would take me a long time to tell you everything, but because of political things that are happening we cannot go out very much. More and more we have had to stay in our room. Mr and Mrs Lehmann seem to be nervous and I think it is because of us. I don't know whether they are breaking a law because I am black – no I think I am Coloured here, which is different, but I don't understand really. Mr and Mrs Lehmann talk about it being like when ordinary people in Austria used to hide Jews from the Nazis, so that they did not get taken away and locked up and were never seen again and then the people who hid them were sometimes shot. I don't think it is quite the same as that, but it makes them very nervous anyway. So Hugh and I stay in our room most of the time and I think this is what started Hugh having his panics again and now it is not always at night that they come. During the day as well he sometimes seems to be somewhere else in his mind and if I try to help he might fly into a rage and go to a corner of the room and cut himself off from me. Then I just have to leave him and wait. When he comes back he seems to know what has happened and he is very sorry and very upset but, John, I think he is starting to believe he cannot get better and he is starting to give up.

Yesterday Mr Lehmann asked me to think about moving on. He said he had been talking with friends and they thought we should go to East London now, which is on the way to Matatiele, and where they know someone who has a hotel by the sea. It is called the Beach Hotel and it has rooms out of the way at the back for staff where we would be safer and not attract attention. You remember East London, John, it is connected with my grandmother and Harry. So we are moving next week because one of Mr Lehmann's group has to go to East London by car. It is a long way but we cannot go by bus – maybe not even go on the same bus – because we could not sit together and it would not be safe for me to leave Hugh sitting on his own.

I am sorry that this is such a long explanation, but I am scared because I don't know what to do when he is ill and I am scared because he is giving up. I need you to tell me what to do. No, I need you. Sorry. I should not have said that.

I hope you can understand something from all this. Perhaps I just needed to tell someone and I have no-one else to tell.

I hope you are well. Please do not mind me contacting you. I hope your other patients are easier than us.

Ndikhumbula wena, Nobomi

ndiyakuthanda...

John

If you have found this, you will probably think it's a bit strange. It's a kind of journal, I suppose. It's reflective, but not in an as-you-go-along sort of way because everything has happened. Finished (in the sense of moved past). And it's my journal, so why write it in the third person, you will say? Why call myself 'he'? Well, it came out that way quite naturally, without thinking about it, without really noticing, and then I realised that the reason was sub-conscious, but that didn't make it any less valid, I thought. The things that happened in those few days, affected me like nothing else ever had, or has since. So I think I used 'he', in order that I could get some sort of clarity, otherwise I would not have been able to see beyond my own emotions. Perhaps I also used 'he' so that I could feel a little more distanced from some of my actions, which, in other circumstances, I might have questioned. But none of that matters now because the thread of life has gathered more staple and goes on spinning.

It was its own world. We were, that is. A very small world, just three people, who each, in their different ways loved each other deeply. At first I thought that the world had ended there, but perhaps it didn't, perhaps it simply metamorphosed. Maybe that's what worlds do, they don't end, they metamorphose.

You can decide for yourself…

"When her second letter came he was immediately engulfed by a whirlwind of conflicting emotions, which had thrown him completely off balance for a couple of days before he had even tried to confront practicalities. Perhaps he genuinely believed he had been engaged in a rational assessment of pros and cons and means, but during the long periods of enforced inaction on the voyage from Southampton, he had finally admitted to having deluded himself if he had thought that there was ever going to be any other outcome. That was not a comfortable admission. If I were a religious man — he had thought on several occasions — I would have to confess and atone in some way. Maybe that thought in itself was a godsend. The atonement could only be to hold to the precious ethic of a doctor (which he knew he was not, and therefore no need to feel bound by their code, but that of course was a specious argument because he knew an ethic such as that of a doctor was clearcut. He hoped.) Many times during those languid hours on deck or ensconced in a corner of the saloon, he had wished his internal saboteur would give up the battle. Of course, he knew it was easier to commit to the honest and honourable course when shielded from moral turmoil by a disinterested Ocean and this maritime cosseting – 'but it won't be so easy when you land', it niggled.

_____

She was on the quayside. He knew she would be, even though he had said he would find his own way to the Beach Hotel. She was behind the crowd in a space on her own – did she want to make sure he didn't miss her?... there was no chance of that – she was wearing an eye-catching white dress with black designs, quite long, without sleeves, a sheen on dark brown arms, alluring, slender, striking, yes, very striking, her curly black hair in short fine plaits taken up into a bunch on top of her head, her look restrained, composed, watching... he was still on the companion-way, he raised his arm and waved hesitantly, he thought she saw him but she did not wave back, just looked his way. He felt a fool. His 'doctor' was fighting with his schoolboy admirer still – neither had enough experience, but he knew which one had to win, he was here to do a job, to save a life perhaps, he could not be distracted. Metaphorically he strapped his arm to his side as he bustled through the crowd;

there could be no expectant peering over heads on tiptoe, no excited rushing to be close...

"I am very pleased to see you again, John, thank you, thank you from both of us."

"I am very pleased you knew to ask."

They were walking down the road which ran behind the passenger quay and its associated buildings. There was a strong wind in their faces. The town appeared to be up to their left and they were walking back towards the river mouth and the open sea, but that was all he could tell. He felt completely disorientated. The wind grew stronger as they approached what he assumed would be some kind of beach. He was relieved that he had brought little to carry with him, the remainder of his possessions having had their sojourn negotiated, at the expense of rash promises of an early return, with Mariana at the hostel. But it was already becoming increasingly difficult to believe that Vienna was any longer on his life-path. The road had turned left as it neared the coast. The wind blowing off the sea was very fresh. He did some mental visualising and calculating to work out the direction. He decided it must be northerly. And quite cold. That surprised him. This was the Indian Ocean and he was walking on African soil. He felt adrift and realised how little he knew about the world that was in the blood of the young woman walking beside him.

"Would you like us to talk about how things have been, before we are together again the three of us?"

"No. Hugh knows you are coming. He was pleased. He promised not to leave the hotel until I got back."

The wind was almost gusting now. He looked out to sea, but turned back quite quickly, bowing his head for shelter.

"We are staying at the Beach Hotel, but we have to be careful. Segregation is fairly rigid in East London. This town was difficult for black people from early on, and most white people see me as Black even though I am Coloured. But the hotel is owned by a friend of the Lehmanns. He is taking a risk for us, though."

"Why are you here, if there could be somewhere easier?"

"That will come. We will tell you. We are nearly there."

He could see a large chalet-style, but quite grand, Victorian building a little way ahead on the other side of the road. It stood slightly above road level and had a colonnade along the front. To him it seemed a bit municipal with its cupola atop the conical roof section which was over the main door. Across the road from the hotel was a grassy slope which gave way to a rocky outline above a narrow beach.

As they approached, Nobomi explained: "You can go to reception, there is a booking for you and they will not want money. Let them take you to your room. I will find out where you are and come to collect you and bring you to where we are. I will leave it for about an hour and then I will come and collect you."

They were coming up the path to the entrance and Nobomi walked away from him, following another path around the side of the building. He went on up to the entrance with a vague feeling of being part of something clandestine. "That shouldn't feel so foreign," he mused, "given that I've just come from the spy capital of Europe." But he couldn't escape the sense of being bounced around like a juggler's ball. Just over three weeks ago he had been at the hostel in Vienna; having negotiated his leave of absence he had travelled to London by train and then to Southampton; then his first experience on a steamer and a very uncomfortable 18-day passage, uncomfortable partly because of bad weather and rough seas almost all the way (or so it seemed) and partly because he had misguidedly chosen second class rather than pay for first class; finally (and with relief) back on terra firma, but on this foreign shore, landing in a place which could have been an English seaside town of fifty years ago, but very definitely wasn't. Now alone in an old-fashioned guest-room in a dated sea-front hotel a long way from anything that was familiar to him, waiting for the woman who was always in his dreams, to lead him... to lead him where? All he knew was that he felt as out of his depth as that first morning around 3 years ago when they had made him 'the doctor'.

Nobomi reappeared in an hour, as she had said. She looked apprehensive.

"John, I don't want you to feel disappointed, as if all your work with Hugh, no, with us, didn't help at all and nothing changed. It did help and we believed, we still believe, that no-one else would have made a difference for us like you did. We are still sure of that." She paused. "We can't really believe that you said you would come. We asked ourselves, why would you? But we can't expect you to tell us that." She paused again. "We know that you will have given up so much to come to us."

"I hope I might be able to work it out myself one day, what told me I had to come, and then I will tell you. But that is for another time. I would like to meet Hugh."

"He has changed. Nothing happened for a long time. But then quite suddenly. Now you will find him different. That's what I wanted to say. I will take you now."

They walked down corridors, through doors, up stairs – he realised they were going towards the rear of the building, perhaps into a wing or annexe – but finally she led him through a rather battered door, opening into a sitting room which seemed to have another smaller room adjoining.

Hugh seemed much diminished from the man he had known, even though he had never known him as the fully fit soldier he must once have been. He did his best to show a welcome to 'the doctor', but it clearly took all his energy. There was the lethargy of a very depressed man and the eyes which saw but did not respond to what they saw.

He knew he was down-hearted at what confronted him, disappointed even, though that of course was not appropriate to his role. He wondered whether he should not first ask for a chronological account from Nobomi of how they came to this point, but he realised that would be grasping for things to 'do' to 'be a doctor'. He also knew he was wanting to understand the relationship in front of him, which had saved this man's life, in Vienna certainly, and perhaps again here, and yet seemed not to be romantic or sexual.

"I sometimes found," his father was saying in his head, "that simply to change the surroundings could be helpful, I think because it introduces new elements. Then in the end the mind reaches out and grasps something from what it sees. It doesn't matter how little a thing."

"I think we should go out, take a walk, talk a little, sit, perhaps, if the wind doesn't make it too cold. Will you get ready and join me in front of the hotel in a few minutes?"

"We will," Nobomi nodded.

––––––––––––

They walked on along the Esplanade. The wind had dropped a little and it was warmer in the early afternoon sunshine. There were a few people around, but, being mid-week and not a holiday, only a few. They walked past the seafront paraphernalia of cafes and guest-houses, shops and holiday stalls to where the road went away from the front and became tree-lined as it skirted the end of the cemetery. They sat among the trees and listened to the drone of the Ocean's waves breaking on the shore.

He was wondering – why this place? why come to East London? Then he heard Nobomi saying almost to herself, "I wonder if my grandfather is really here?"

Both men looked up unsure how to respond.

He thought – is that why we are in this town?

He said: "You never told me very much about your grandfather."

"Grandmother did not speak about him. Only occasionally. It hurt her too much, I think. She loved him so much, she would never love again – I heard her say that to my mother. And once when I asked her how she could fall in love with him when he wasn't Xhosa like she was, she said a funny thing, she said no-one had ever called her **Miss** Nobomi before. What did she mean?"

"Perhaps she realised she was completely ok for him."

"He saw she was a long way from home and on her own and wouldn't charge her for sending the message to her family."

Reflecting again she said, "I found out more from Louie, the funny English lady that found us in Stephansplatz. I didn't even know his name until Louie told me, but I think there were things that she didn't tell me too." She was thoughtful for a moment. Then, wistfully, "He drowned. Just out there." She was looking out to sea. "But he shouldn't have drowned, he was a good swimmer. And now," he thought there was moistness in her eyes, "he's in there somewhere." She turned in the direction of the cemetery.

"Do you think we could find his grave? Before you leave us, John. I think there's something else, you see. Perhaps it was what Louie wouldn't tell me."

Hugh had been listening calmly, watching her all the time, never shifting his gaze from her face. She returned the attention and smiling she said, "Thank you Hugh".

He knew there must be more.

They walked back slowly to the Beach Hotel and he joined them later in their rooms for the meal that Nobomi had arranged.

———————————

He was accustomed to sleeping soundly and it was certain that he would that night after 2 weeks or so of restless slumber lashed by the relentless swell of the Atlantic, then, on rounding the Cape thrown around on the currents of the Indian Ocean – to think that he felt a romantic twinge when he read its florid name on the map back in Vienna! – and then a day bewildered at the incongruity of a kind of Englishness on this very foreign continent... so tonight he would sink into dreamless silent oblivion.

The hammering on his door started sometime after 3. He was working backwards in his mind to find the time, when he surfaced far enough to realise that this pounding noise the propellers were making coming out of the water as the boat plunged into the next trough had been going on since the man in the bunk above his had started moaning between bouts of retching. But it was only when one foot touched the floor and the floor stayed level that it became clear to him that he wasn't any longer on the boat. Still only hazily conscious of where this new room belonged, he lurched towards the door and grabbed it open, causing Nobomi, who was becoming frantic in her knocking, to fall hard against him, pinning him to the wall. He felt her curly black hair, now loose, brushing against his neck, he felt her warmth, the hand poised to hit the door now resting supple on his shoulder, in the confusion of the yielding door one of her legs was now between his legs... and for an instant everything was motionless, then he felt her body relax... or... yield?... no, not yield, relax, just relax, he must... he blinked hard several times, stiffened his body against her weight and gently distanced her from his vulnerability. Now he could see her face. She wore a look of desperation.

"It's Hugh. Please come. I don't think I can hold him."

When they burst into the room Hugh was lying on the floor curled into the fœtus position alternately moaning and gasping for breath with hands clenched and arms tautened over his head. He must have been like this since Nobomi had left the room. Shortly after they arrived, still unaware of their presence, the agonising body rolled over and stretched out on its back, legs writhing and hands pressed hard over face and forehead.

"Lie down alongside him," he said, "just close enough so that he will know you are there. Be very still."

- from somewhere a hazy picture came into his mind, a frightened mother with her child -

Nobomi lay down, and he sat on the other side, not quite so close, but close enough so that when Hugh came back he could be seen and be felt listening.

For almost an hour they waited.

When the eyes seemed to be focusing, he asked: "Will you tell me how it began, Hugh?"

"She would never love again... I've taken that away from her... Can't go back now... the War... where is she now?... do you know?..." Hugh drifted away and his eyes glazed over.

He looked across to Nobomi: "Could you bring some covers from the bed?" Nobomi went to the bedroom and came back with two blankets. Hugh fell asleep as they were wrapping the bedclothes around.

He knew he had to leave them. He was struggling to remain the 'doctor' they had made him, but he could, so long as... she didn't come too close... no, no, he had to go. Now. It would be alright, Hugh was likely to sleep for a few hours. He gave her an encouraging smile as he whispered "Well done", quietly left, and wound his way back along the corridors to his own room.

———————————

"I have been talking to the hotel manager and he advised that it would be better if you did not come to the Municipal Offices with us to find out about the cemetery and where your grandfather is buried." The three of them were in the room again much later in the morning. "He said that officials were unpredictable at the moment because of the general state of unrest over the efforts to clear remaining Africans and Coloureds out of the main town and up to a Location. I think that's right."

He had been worried about broaching this with Nobomi: it was not in his nature to give any thought to colour, to the point where he was simply unaware, but his initially quite casual conversation with the manager that morning had alerted him and now he felt awkward and naïve. He was in a quandary. Hugh had recovered well enough from his episode during the night and was wanting to come with him – he could see no reason why not, and it could give him a chance to understand more about the cause of the distress during the night – but for the two of them to go and leave Nobomi felt a little like playing to the very segregation politics which he felt as so repugnant here. And then there was his own fumbling and confusion when he came close to her. To his relief she made it easy for him...

"It would be helpful if you would go with Hugh because I know he wants to talk to you and maybe that will be easier if you are walking together. The manager says I can use the little room at the front under the tower which has a view over the Ocean. It will remind me of when we sat up in the attic room in Vienna looking out over the city."

He felt he had been let off. He was relieved. A little later the two men left the Beach Hotel by the front door. They turned towards the port as they went out of the hotel and then took the second road leading away from the sea because it appeared to be the busier one and heading for the centre. This was Fitzpatrick Road and in less than a quarter of a mile they walked past number 45, where Nobomi's grandmother had been living with Harry a little over 50 years before, at the time he drowned. If the sea breeze gusted behind them at that moment and they shivered briefly, they did not notice.

It took them a little over a quarter of an hour to reach the Town Hall. It had seemed natural to walk at a good pace setting out, but as they walked up Oxford Street, with its assortment of shops and professional offices and the occasional small workshop part concealed down its own alleyway, their pace slowed – was it the sense of a stage nearing its end, or the darkness growing from this shadow of a past which was enveloping all three companions and would leave its trace on each like a smooth-worn grain slightly proud on a timber seat? The Town Hall, with its pared-down Victorian grandeur and slightly too tall clock tower, which seemed to emulate St Stephen's Tower (though no Big Ben was housed here), stood in formal welcome. The usual stone-flagged corridors lurked inside, wide and ponderous on the ground floor, gradually narrowing with each floor and their distance from the main staircase.

They indicated their purpose to the clerk in the registry section on the third floor and were asked to wait. After a few minutes they were shown into the office of the deputy registrar, who explained that it was not common to be asked for information from as long ago as the beginning of the century, but if they could wait a few moments he would seek out the files. He ceremoniously opened a double-doored cupboard built into one wall and started searching through shelves of heavily bound volumes with green spines. He pulled out one and then started searching the shelves on the other side and finally pulled out another from those with red binding.

"Here we are, gentlemen. You say the family name was Cole and his Christian name was Harry." He started leafing through one of the books which seemed to contain counterfoils of certificates. After a few moments he looked up, "I think this will be the one, the grave space was purchased by one R. Symons Cole. The grave number is 592.5C and it is in the new cemetery. Fortunately, my predecessor of 50 or so years ago has written the name Harry as its first occupant and after that there is no other name, so we can assume that he is the only one. If you are intending to go and look for the grave, 5C is the section and 592 is the number of the grave within the section. But I think you will need to find the caretaker to help you, gentlemen." He went on, "Also you might be interested in the entry in the register. I should be able to find it now we have an exact date." Some leafing through pages in the other volume and then a triumphant deputy registrar held out for them a faded page of hand-written entries in the large and rather dog-eared ledger.

The page was headed "Death Notice" and its 'owner' clearly shown as the deceased Harry Cole. He was eighteen years and two months old when he died and he had been the telegraph clerk at the Post Office. The circumstances of his death were just about readable: "Drowned while bathing from beach East London, body washed ashore at a spot near Beach Hotel ... (unreadable) ... 3rd May 1902"

Seeing both men fall silent, the official sensitively excused himself. For both, standing in the office of the Deputy Registrar in the Town Hall of East London on a continent neither would have expected ever to visit, there was the same incredulity that this death more than 50 years before had made them companions at a watershed in both their lives.

"We don't keep a plan of the graves here," said the Deputy Registrar who had cautiously returned, "but if you go to the office at the main entrance of the cemetery, a groundsman will direct you. You should not expect anything elaborate. There is not likely to be a headstone, it will more likely be an unmarked patch of ground. But we do our best to keep things tidy. You can leave your own remembrance, but nothing permanent, you understand – for that you need permission from this office.

———————————

"Reading the Death Notice just now," he said as they sat down on one of the benches along a quiet part of the Esplanade on their way back to the hotel, "it seemed to bring together many strands, even though we don't know what they are, just that somehow they are all linked."

Then, "Should we talk about last night?"

"You are the one who carries on," Hugh said.

He took a moment to reply, struggling to grasp the meaning of what he had heard.

"Can we not all carry on, the three of us?"

"No."

He had a sense that Hugh saw clearly how everything was going to work out. A far-off memory appeared in his mind: he was at a school sports day, lining up on the starting line for the cross-country race, waiting for "Go", his best friend, the real champion but injured this time, standing by and encouraging him. At the first turn in the course he had looked back and he saw his friend walking away head down. He knew he must win, but he had felt no elation.

Hugh went on: "There are not just three. There are four. There will always be four. I told you about Barbara, you remember? I ruined her life and I cannot put that right. She waited and I did not come. I cannot allow myself to do it again. Not with Nobomi. She will not leave me unless I am well. But I cannot be well. You cannot see how my mind is changed. But I know. The prison, those years. That vile cell. I see it every night. And I cannot make it different. I am out of the prison, but there is no release for me."

He waited, and then: "Do you believe I am here to take her away?"

Hugh looked up, "No, you could not take her until she wanted to go. I could not even make her go myself. But she must. I will ruin her life, like Barbara, because I cannot change, and I am poison. I can't, not again."

He knew how it could be when hope faded, like a view slowly bleached of all features by a blinding sun. Emptied of its content, the mind has nothing to turn to, its domain an infinity of emptiness. The only prospect, endless waiting. But no peace. It was a place of danger. He knew that too. His father had told him how the final reckoning could come suddenly and unexpectedly, you had to watch for the easing of the despair, he had said, too often it is a false trail.

"But not quite yet," said Hugh suddenly, "no, not yet. There is something else about the grave."

For a moment he wondered if Hugh had caught the thoughts inside his own head, but then he realised that no, what he had heard was not for him, and he regretted he had lost contact with his patient, his companion.

————————————

At the Beach Hotel, they found Nobomi in the attic room below the tower, still gazing out over the Ocean. He had copied all the entries from the page of the Death Notice and he gave this to her. She read through his written sheet and sat silently for a while. Then, looking out again over the Ocean, she said, "It all happened here. It has been around us all the time. They were in this hotel.

"I must go down to the sea, to where they found him." He made to gather their things to accompany her, but she said, "No, I will go alone."

She left the room and minutes later they saw her walking straight from the front of the hotel, to the surprise of guests and the alarm of trailing receptionists. She crossed the road, went down over the grass bank, finally tracing a path over the rocky shoreline which led down to the sea. She stood above the breaking waves looking out

to the horizon, her arms at her sides, a dark
silhouette against the foaming of the waves and
the sea glinting in the sun.

He wasn't sure how long she stood there, how
long they were watching her from the attic room,
but the time had a tranquillity and a communion
which he would always recall, though he would
never experience it in the same way again.

When she returned, she simply said, "I would like
to go to my grandfather's grave tomorrow. Can we
do that?" They agreed, of course, they would go
in the morning and, if it was not too windy, they
would walk along the Esplanade again to get
there.

———————

The day was overcast but not cold. There was a
gentle breeze blowing onshore. The sea was
heaving restlessly, but there were no plumes of
spray to be seen. They walked on the shoreside
and you might have been struck by their air of
purposefulness, but remember they were
following their tracks of a couple of days before.
Perhaps you would have thought three friends
out for a walk on such a morning would have had
more to exchange, but they did not talk. Perhaps
you might have wondered about their purpose.

Where the shoreline started to curve eastwards
they took a well-used track through the brush
and scrubland which brought them to the back of
the cemetery. He was not prepared for its
appearance, coming from a country where the
ritual of death required formality if not reverence
– graveyards often in the precincts of holy places,

burial grounds neatly ordered and surrounded by walls with ornate railings and impressive gates. It was not anything like that. Coming to the edge of the scrubland on this side, it was not clear where the boundary was, for there was no fence, rather a change of vegetation and then you realised that you might be walking over graves which were not simply unmarked but overgrown.

It occurred to him that such a burial place was fitting for this country of vast open spaces and outback scrubland, for it was flat and extended far into the distance with one central track lined on each side with what he believed were spruce trees. Beyond this, on both sides a carpet of poorly-tended grass interspersed at irregular intervals by the occasional low tree with a bulbous head of leafy foliage of the type which were what he could imagine you see on an African prairie. On a clear day with a blue sky, and the stillness in this place, he imagined the feeling would be one of peace at life's journey's end, a reward of undisturbed repose. But today was not such a day, for the sky was grey and seemed menacing in its darker tones. Stillness but no peace, he thought. Brooding rather than resting.

The central passageway was straight as an arrow, an avenue flanked by the tall spruce, stretching out of sight. As far as he could see, the whole cemetery was deserted, its aspect, a latterly curated park slowly reverting to nature, but dotted with a variety of stone pillars, the leftover markers of the departed. It gave him a strange sense of a world waiting, unknowing in its

stillness, on the edge of void, deserted by life.
Almost. In the far distance there was a solitary
figure standing in the centre of the pathway.
From where they were it seemed still, but as
they got closer they could see it was
approaching. A man, he thought, a big man too –
but how could he know that, when the figure was
still so far off? They were moving slowly towards
the middle of the grounds, where the layout of
the paths formed a circle around the crossing –
he thought such a symbolic design would be more
advantageously viewed from above – walking
towards the centre of the cross and on to where
they would join the circle again. Perhaps it was
their interest in the design distracted them, but
suddenly he was there facing them. The man had
stopped a few yards ahead and now it was clear
from his clothes that he was a gardener or
perhaps the caretaker. They were a little startled
and he had a strange sense of this large man and
the cemetery he cared for being one. Xhosa, he
presumed. The man said nothing and was looking
at them without concern. It is interesting, he
thought, how so often large men are placid. He
thought of his grandfather. The man looked at
each of them in turn, for a few seconds it
seemed, spending longest on Nobomi. She asked
him in Xhosa for the sector which was 5C. He
turned to their right and without speaking
indicated the large area which abutted the track.
She thanked him. He did not respond, but walked
on slowly between them and continued in the
direction from which they had come. They looked
from one to the other in the way people do when
they are fumbling for the next move, then back

down the track past the crossing, perhaps in the
hope of more directions, but the man was
nowhere to be seen. They noticed that the breeze
had dropped and the air was completely still and
seemed to cling. It was probably the slight
unease of this that spurred them into action.
They left the track on the side the man had
indicated and saw they were in an area more
than 50 yards square which was bounded by a
narrow pathway on which the grass seemed to be
shorter and worn down with use. Beyond and to
either side were similar squares and beyond
those, others. They started to wander between
the burial plots, which had a uniformity of
spacing though not form, for some had
headstones, some had informal memorials in
various styles, mostly of rough stone or wood, and
some were unmarked: those you could only guess
from their position. The grass and other foliage,
though, had not recently been cut – might they
be walking on graves? – and the whole had an air
of neglect. Was the man the only custodian of
this place?

Walking around was tiring and their increasing
sense of the impossibility of their search – there
must have been many more than 100 graves in
each square – was wearying. Without any
particular intention, they had drifted apart, the
two men towards the far side of the square,
Nobomi now down towards the crossing. The gloom
of the day was hanging heavy and more than
once he tripped over hidden roots or was tangled
by vines. Looking down so much of the time to
try to avoid such snares, he had not noticed a
dark silhouette which had appeared on one side

of their square. Did he hear it first, or did he look across in the instant her terror struck? Nobomi on her knees, transfixed, her head in her hands, and a terrified scream "Nooooooooooo......." which he knew instantly, for he had heard it once before. In the same moment that he saw her, he saw the dark silhouette just beyond her, arm raised, holding a hooked tool... about to strike... There was an instant when he couldn't move, the scream seemed to occupy the whole world, then he was running, stumbling, colliding with headstones, another deeper "Noooooo...." – Hugh was just behind him – he was running with all his strength and still so far... but finally there, collapsing at her side, not daring to touch her, to break her fragile shield. He looked up, and the man from the track had dropped his arm, motioning towards the grave which he had been clearing with a sickle for them. Lying on the ground was a simple wooden cross, well-aged, but you could still make out, carved along the cross-piece, one name –

HARRY

Leaning close to her, he said softly, "Not a mbulu this time, he is your friend."

Looking at these four people so still around a grave, silhouettes all, now, under a glowering sky, you might have felt you were viewing a sculpture. Very faintly you might have heard the drone of the waves breaking on the shore, but for these few minutes, this world was motionless.

Gradually, very gradually, Nobomi began to relax. She looked up at the man and said, "Thank you, I remember. It is over now. I am free."

After a moment, and without knowing where the words came from, "You were there, weren't you?"

He thought he saw the man's face relax a little, as if some great weight had just been lifted. He had put aside his sickle and knelt down at the head of the grave just to one side. Now there was only Nobomi and the man in the world. Leaning forward, looking solemnly into her eyes, he put a hand on the grave and said, awkwardly but clearly, "Harry". Then he placed his other hand on the ground to the side and whispered, "Ngoxolo".

Tears began to stream down her face and fall to the ground, but there were no sobs, there was no heaving in distress, just tears... he thought, 'this is truly relief, it **is** over at last, her world can finally be at peace.

He was not aware how long they stayed like that but when they looked up, the man had gone.

Nobomi took off a wrist braid she always wore and buried it in the grass over where her mother lay, then kneeled for a few moments between the two graves, the one that was meant to be and the other that was not, and laid a hand on each, then bent her head over and with her forehead touched the earth between.

When finally she stood up she looked at Hugh: "I wonder how he knew. I didn't tell him the number of the grave."

Hugh said, "Perhaps that will be another day."

A little later, they made their way slowly and silently back to the Beach Hotel.

————————————

They ate together that evening, as had become their custom, in the rooms at the back of the hotel. Somehow he knew that they would have talked through the night after he had left them to return to his own room, though she never told him what about and he knew he would never ask. Before he had left their room, he had stood facing Hugh and they had looked into each other's eyes, openly, expressively, intimately; no words had passed, for words have no place at such a time; then he had slightly bowed his head in recognition before turning to leave.

He woke as it was getting light and she was standing looking out over the Ocean – every night after that first one he had left the door unlocked, in case of an emergency, he told himself. He had no idea how long she had been there. She seemed to be gazing intently, far out, but she turned when she heard him stir and walking slowly over, she said, "Hugh has left us." Then she took off her nightgown, lifted the sheet and lay naked down beside him. After a while she turned to him on her side, rested her head on his shoulder and put her arm around him.

Sometime later they made love.

————————————

"Hugh left a note for you." They were sitting on the grass bank opposite the hotel, above the shore. She handed him a double-folded sheet. "Here it is. I don't know what it says."

Dear John,

I believe that you will understand why I am going to take this course. I think you knew, when we sat and talked on the way back from the Town Hall, but of course as doctor you could not allow anything so wilful to be part of your vision. This is the path that Harry walked, I am sure. The circumstances look different fifty years on, but that is only outward appearance. We both reached the point where there is only one way to release someone who can only be who they are if you can also be who you are. For Harry, and now for me, this was all that was left.

I could not hold Nobomi back from finding her grandmother, but she would not have been able to do that with me, because she would not have left me. She will do it now with you and the thought of that makes me very happy. Yes, I mean that: at my end I will be happy. But I needed to wait until we found the grave. I was sure there was something else, and there was, she found her mother. Harry's daughter. I hope when you find the first Nobomi, she will tell you the whole story, how it was possible and who was the black mbulu – yes, I have heard Nobomi's dream too. I believe it has laid to rest our Nobomi's evil spirit.

John, you have been a true companion and used your skills selflessly. I thank you with all my heart for getting me this far. You were never going to be able to bring me back to health, but I hope sincerely you will not be tortured by that. You deserve to walk away from here with a light heart – yes, I mean that too. And Nobomi deserves to have her man a confident companion.

Thank you for everything,

Hugh

PS. Did you want to know what 'ndiyakuthanda' means? It means 'I love you'

―――――――――――

It was a few days later before he and Nobomi left East London for Matatiele. They had to wait to obtain permits to travel, and because Adam's friend was certain that it would be safer not to take the direct route via Umtata but to go by train to Maclear. This was in livestock country in the foothills of the Drakensberg, where most of the people were Xhosa. They would be able to obtain horses and a guide, and then they could follow the mountain route and come to Matatiele from the north. It would be an arduous journey, but it would mean that they would be accepted and in country remote enough not to be troubled by the Afrikaner bands.

One morning sitting on the shore watching the sun rise, he had noticed that he had lost any expectation that his life 'should' be on a particular course that he might be able to define as a purpose or a goal. But this did not feel uncomfortable — why should he be in any hurry? — why should he even have to know? Life could simply take its course — that's what Harry would have said. He realised that he was pondering, though, on whether they should delay their departure from East London, until the sea gave Hugh back, but Nobomi told him, "He won't be found."

He wondered how she knew.

On 15th November 1954 they left East London for Matatiele.

———————————

from the author's journal…

Do we have a right over our own life to the extent of being able to choose to end it? Who can say we don't? If there is a God and that God says life is sacred, we have no right… but what if the pain is too great?… and who can assess 'too great' except we ourselves? The ultimate duality of Life & Death produces a Black & White argument and uncrossable lines – always very seductive because we don't have to take responsibility. Ubuntu tradition holds that "I can only be me, if you can be you" – there is still a line, but to know where that line is, requires dialogue.

So what was said that last night when Hugh and Nobomi were together and talked into the night? We can only presume that he convinced her he would not get better. "Hugh has left us" and "He won't be found". It sounded like a mutual resignation.

Ubuntu is a kind of co-dependence. Western thinking, we shy away from from that notion, but… this way we have to keep on talking.

umzukulwana wam…

Bathandwa

There was rumours of occasional sightings long time 'fore we really knew anything. You know how it is, one person says something in conversation and that starts off a memory for someone else which hadn't meant nothing at all at the time, and they pass it on, then another person remembers something, and that would never have connected neither, but slowly a story starts to grow. Then people are looking to find things. Thinking back, the first I heard was from a friend of my brother who 'ad gone to Maclear to collect some cattle coming by train and he was talking to the guard who said he'd let two passengers travel in his van from Sterkstroom, had to keep quiet about it – it wasn't a passenger line by that time you see – an English man and a Xhosa girl, least he thought she was

Xhosa but she might have been Coloured, didn't say where they were going at first, just said they needed horses. He told them where to find Khwezi's kraal, then they said they needed a guide to take them to Matatiele by the mountain track. He thought they was crazy, said it would take them least a week and likely much longer, but if anyone could find a guide 'twould be Khwezi, might even go with them hisself if it suited him. Two travellers on horses, that's why I remembered it you see, I thought it could 'ave been them as I'd seen on the mountainside as I was bringing the herd over this year. Then there was the lonesome hunter or herder that came down from the mountains and said they'd seen a couple of strangers. One stayed a night with them and said there was a white man about 30 and a young Xhosa woman. He thought they must be lost but they said they weren't, just that their guide had needed to go back to Maclear. He remembered the girl's name – Nobomi. Now, that started me thinkin' e'en more, because I know a Nobomi, here in Matatiele. Not just me, everyone knows Nobomi. It's not a big place, but you know how it is, sometimes you get someone who seems to stand for a place, like a celebrity you would say. Well this old lady was one of those. Must have been well into her seventies, almost blind, but she still lived on her own, just outside the town on th'edge of the Location on the hillside, she had a traditional round *ikhava* with a small shanty built on. When word had started getting around 'bout her past and it seemed she was someone notable, the council tried to get her to move to the edge of town, they offered her a free house, but she wouldn't take it. She said she was in her family's house that she had left when she was 15 to walk to the Ocean, and she had come back to complete a circle. I don't think that was the reason – how could she have remembered which house it was after 50 years? – nay, I think it was principle, and pride. Us Blacks are not allowed to live in the town, that's the apartheid regulations, but I think there were a few on the council felt guilty – not all Whites agreed with the regulations – and being the council they wanted to keep the peace. So they would 'ave put her right on the edge of town, probably moved the boundary, and pretended they believed in doing right by everybody. Anyway, she stayed put where she was. There were all sorts of stories about her, I think when she dies she will be a legend. Some say she took on the municipality at Port Elizabeth, and someone who came from there was sure she had been in that riot when all those people were killed. And the African unions resistance, when that started she was in that somehow, she might even have been one of those activists who went to prison. They knew 'bout her in Umtata as well; there they thought she was with an Englishman down in East London and had a daughter. But up here even those that knew 'er well and visited 'er a lot said she never talked about any family 'cept the family she had left behind here in Matatiele all those years before. You'd have thought if she had had a daughter, she'd have said something to someone, wouldn't you?

Over the next few days I kept wondering whether that hunter's story had got to her ears. I thought about going to her place and telling her myself, but I didn't really know her like that and with her having this status in people's minds, well, that made me nervous a bit. That's silly, I suppose, because people who do know her say she listens and just lets everyone be as they are.

Perhaps you're wondering how it could be that a whole story could have built up about those two people before they arrived, when most news comes by word of mouth in these parts and the ones carrying it had to get around same way as the travellers themselves. But you have to remember that is how things are here. 'Course there's telephones and the wireless and a few even have television, that's the Whites of course, but this is Africa and we talk about anything that's happening. I was the first person who heard the story from the herder because he'd needed some help with an injured cow calving, so I went out. Anyway, he said he didn't think they were in no hurry. He'd asked them why they were going to Matatiele. The girl said, "I came from there a long time ago". 'E asked her how long ago because he might know someone she knew, and she thought for a bit, like she was working it out, then she said, "I think it was over 50 years ago." Well that was it, he didn't ask 'er anything else after that, I think 'e was a bit scared — "she looked 20, Bathandwa, how could she've left here 50 years ago?" You would prob'ly say he was the superstitious sort, but you've got to remember that our older people think the ancestors are watching us and we believe that they can be angry sometimes. Our healers make contact with the ancestors to bring healing, and they can appear in different ways. So when she said that, poor Thandiwe just wanted to get away. But you can imagine how the story grew as it got told around. Mm, suppose that was my part. I started it. The older kids who looked after the sheep got to riding up into the hills to try and get sight o' them. In the end, it was like the whole place was holding its breath. When were they going to appear? Even the Whites was talkin' about it. But her name didn't get into the story. Nobomi, that is. I think I was the only one knew her name because that hunter was not from here and he was going up into Basuto when I met him. And with it being Nobomi, I thought I shouldn't tell it.

It was a few weeks since the story first was bein' told and I 'ad stopped thinkin' about it because things had started to die down a bit, you know how it is, if rumours aren't fed they lose their energy. Well I had been in town and they had asked me at the Butchery if I would take a parcel to Nobomi because their delivery boy was ill. So here I was, on my way up to her place which was on the open grassland beside the road over to Jabavu. It was a good place up on the veldt as it rises into the hills. You could look down and see the town and way way beyond there was the Ocean, but you couldn't see that far of course, you just knew it was there somewhere past the horizon. She invited me in. I told you I didn't really think I knew her, but she's one of those people who seem to want to be friendly to everyone. And I was thinking I might be able to help her with something, her being almost blind. But she didn't need help. She made me sit down with her outside and gave me a beer – yes, she brewed beer, illegal of course under the regulations for us Blacks to brew beer, but there was no policeman was going to arrest Nobomi. She said she wanted to talk to me because she had heard that my father had worked in East London. I told her that he was there when he was 18 I thought, and she wanted to know when that was and if he had told me anything about it. I said that it was in the time when the British were fighting the Ibhulu (that's the Xhosa word for Boer), so I thought that was at the beginning of the century. I didn't care to ask why she wanted to know. I just sat and waited for her. She was seeming to be looking out into the distance into the other world. When she spoke, I wasn't sure she was speaking to me, she was still looking into the distance, as if she was seeing a dream: "I walked to East London when I left here, a long long way, more than a year, and then the Ocean, I didn't know that it would be like that." She paused. It was all quiet. I could feel my body completely still. Like suspended. Then: "There was a clerk in the Post Office, my age, he sent a message for me to my family, he called me *Miss* Nobomi." Then she went quiet again. I had been looking at her as she was speaking. She turned to me and skimmed the fingers of one hand over my face like blind people do and said, "You look like your father."

"How do you know that, *usisi omdala*[9], he died many years ago, before you came back to Matatiele?"

"I knew your father," she smiled, "in a drinking place, in East London."

One of my father's stories suddenly came to life in my memory. "A drinking place near the sea?"

"*Ewe*[10]. Fitzpatrick Road. He was kind to us."

"You, and…?"

There was another long pause. But the suspense had gone now and I could break the silence…

"He told me about a bar close to the sea. He said it was mainly young people like him who went there, mostly Xhosa. Never Whites, but a young English started coming with a Xhosa girl. He was friendly and confident but not one of those – White boss and all Blacks are 'boys' – he was normal. Like us. My father knew his name – Harry. But his girl never spoke. He always looked after her and did everything for her. It seemed strange, 'e said, her not speaking, because she wa' one of us, Xhosa. But she was very shy with us, even looked scared sometimes. Some of the kids in the bar weren't so nice and they started making jibes and insults because he was the only White lad, said

---

[9] old sister

[10] yes

she was a prostitute and they made accusations like he was trying to pass her off because she was a problem for him, not nice things, and my father, he was a big man, he faced up to the main one and told him people were people and what they didn't know they shouldn't make up. It went alright after that. But he said the girl was still sad all the time and didn't…"

"Not Harry, it was our own."

I was stopped in my tracks. I'd thought I was talking about another world, but I wasn't, she was there, sitting right next to me. It was *her* world.

I stuttered on. "My father said she… you, became happy suddenly, but your man became sad. And then you stopped coming and you never come back. And no-one even knew your name. No-one knew…" My voice gave out on me as the end of the story appeared in my mind.

That seemed to be all. We just sat, looking down, the old *usisi* and her admirer, but Nobomi picked up the story: "Harry was the post office clerk. It was special how he treated me, because I was just a country girl and I was only 17. To have a white boy call me 'Miss', can you imagine? He saw we both knew what it was like to be a long way from home. A bit later he was there again. When I needed someone. He was the only one, in the middle of the night, the men in my house they'd raped me, I ran and I found his rooms and he let me in and just let me stay. He didn't touch me, for a long long time he didn't touch me, like that I mean. We talked. Often. A lot. And I got over what they had done to me. Then I wanted him. I wanted Harry. To heal me, so that I could forget. He did. And I was so happy."

She wavered a little, as if unsure whether to turn a page.

"We had a daughter. But he never saw her. He never saw his daughter, Ngoxolo. The Ocean took him. I knew. He believed we could not be safe if he was there."

Again she wavered.

"Afterwards his brother Frank looked after us for a long time. As a brother. But one day I knew I had to leave. So that Frank could live."

And then…

"Ngoxolo married. A good man. A worthy man. They killed her, his clan. I don't know…"

I had not heard the scuffing up the track, but when people become blind they develop better hearing. Nobomi had heard it. She looked up and gazed towards the sound, contemplating it in the way that people do who cannot see. Suddenly she stood up, her arms stretched in the air and screamed:

"umzukulwana wam"[11]

---

[11] "my granddaughter"

umzukulwana wam…

The horses stopped. They were about 50 yards away. The girl dismounted and was running full tilt towards us, Nobomi set off over the grass – I's afraid she would fall – but they met just in time and, well, you will have to imagine, I don't think I can go on…

~~~

Nothing could have prepared me for this. I was in a different world again, thrown from heartache to rapture. How can this happen? I felt their joy as my own. I wished that if my father was watching this, he would feel it too.

I didn't see the man dismount, so absorbed I was, but then he was coming up behind me and he put his hand on my shoulder and we stood looking on together as those years vanished, and we in our world could only stand and watch. Like favoured guests, this humble herder and his surprise companion.

"Who was the man who showed us where the graves were?"

"That was Uuka. He found me when I arrived in Port Elizabeth with your mother as an infant. He made sure we had somewhere to live and he would not let anyone near us that he thought might harm us. He doesn't talk, but he watches. I knew I could trust him."

"How did he know us?"

"The last time I ever saw you, he was there. But we don't just remember with our eyes. And you were special, because you were Nobomi too, so he was your protector as well."

"I don't know what happened, but the terror has gone now. It was at the grave everything changed. Somehow it was Uuka, but I don't understand... he had a weapon, a kind of claw, as if he was killing..."

"He killed to protect us. He killed the man who had killed your mother."

"I saw I didn't need to be scared all these years. I thanked him. But he disappeared. We didn't see him again."

"He is a good man. He knew his work was finished. That was enough."

"My mother was next to Harry. She was really there?"

"Yes, really. Uuka hid her body and buried her one night. I heard later that he had taken a job at the cemetery to watch until you came."

"He believed I would return one day."

"He believed. He was waiting."

I wondered how you fill a space in your life like this. Watching them and listening, sometimes it seemed like the gap was only 15 years or so – that's about what it must have been since these two Nobomis were last together – but then sometimes it seemed like the gap was much bigger, maybe the 50 years that scared Thandiwe up in the mountains, but when I saw it like that I saw something else as well and for a moment it looked like there weren't two Nobomis at all, just one and... now *I* was scared and I'm not a superstitious type like Thandiwe, I believe in honouring our ancestors but I don't believe they come and change things in our lives, except… except when it happens like this and it looks like something has stayed, something doesn't let go…

"My name is John. Who are you?"

I jumped. I had lost the feeling of the hand on my shoulder, but his hand was still there.

"I am Bathandwa." Then I thought I ought to say something else to be friendly. "My father helped her a long time ago."

"Which one?"

"I'm not sure now. In East London."

"We've come from East London."

"There was a bar in Fitzpatrick Road. They went there. My father went there as well. But they stopped suddenly. Later someone found the boy's body. Drowned. 'You can be just going along,' my father said, 'everything ordinary, and right alongside you there's some big tragedy about to happen.' I always remember him saying that."

I realised that now I knew his name. "Harry. The boy that drowned. He never saw his daughter."

"We went and saw the graves. She is next to him now."

"That's how it should be. Praise be."

"Uuka could not save my mother?"

"He tried, but they had locked him up. He was in time to save you, and me."

"There was another man."

"Adam. He helped us too."

"He found me in Vienna. He said he had brought me to Vienna, but I didn't remember. He would not tell me everything. I think it was about my mother. He said it would be too painful. Was he there?"

"Yes, he was there. I will tell you. He had become one of our group that was trying to get better living conditions for African workers. We were not a union, but we wanted to fight the same battle, just not in a way that was going to get the Whites and Afrikaners scared so that they opposed the cause. The ANC were too soft back then, they had too many Blacks with interests to protect – education, professional jobs, good houses. They thought their Black middle class could get accepted like a White middle class and they would be allowed to be real neighbours in the cities. No sir. Then there were the unions, and in the end the Communist Party, but there were some folk in them who were out to show how great they were and get the ordinary folks worshipping them and making them feel they were powerful. But those types scared the Whites because they used violence and they couldn't see we needed the good Whites to be on our side. So we tried to be in the middle, fight with words, but strong words, passionate words. We wanted *non*-racialism. Black White Coloured Indian Afrikaner Boer British – South Africa, it's like a rainbow really. That's where Adam came in. He was a reporter, no, an editor I think, on the Herald. He put our side in the Newspaper. He was clever. For a long time his bosses didn't realise what he was doing. Then someone found out he was one of us and they sacked him. That was when the trouble was building up. Your father's family were middle class and ANC and they thought he got sent to prison because of your mother, she was one of the violent rabble they thought. But she wasn't. They paid a gang to cause trouble and take revenge. We didn't find out in time. They locked Uuka away and he could not get to us soon enough. When he did they ran. But it was too late. They called the police and said I had done it, killed Ngoxolo – me, kill my own daughter! I think someone bribed the police. They came, lots of them. There was only just time. I begged Adam to take you away as far as he could go, a long way from South Africa. Uuka would not leave me. But I told him that the most important thing for me was that Ngoxolo was decently buried, so he took her body and hid with her until he could bury her. I told him where Harry was, and he said he could get her to East London, but I never really thought he would… I'm so pleased she is with her father…"

Nobomi couldn't go on. She was sobbing. She looked exhausted. I was hearing this for the first time and *I* was shaking.

"And they sent you to prison, for killing the man who killed my mother?"

"Yes. I don't think they believed me, but I refused to speak. So Uuka would be safe. I made him promise not to come back. It was me they wanted and there was no-one else they could find."

"And all the time you did not know where I was?"

"I did not know where you were until... just now."

"I never let go of your locket."

"It's your's now."

The two women shed tears and hugged like they'd never let go.

And us two men? Well, we shed a few tears too.

~~~

How do you celebrate the disappearance of 15 years of wondering, hoping, longing? Or was it 50? I could still not be sure, always an image behind the image. Who *is* Nobomi? But did it matter now the thread was joined up again and could spin on into the invisible future?

Of course, there was a party.

Grandmother Nobomi sent me off with a list of people to find and tell to come that evening, and bring some beer because she hadn't got enough in stock. It took us 2 hours to get right round – yes, me and John, we took the horses – and by the time we got back the track was already filling up with our early stops. If you count whole families there were over 100 on the list, but in these parts word spreads fast, and I think there was much more than 200 came in the end.

The Dragon was blowing a light wind down from its mountain that night. They must have heard us down in Umtata, maybe even all the way to the Ocean.

Epilogue

Letter from Nobomi to Louie 31st December 1955

Matatiele, Eastern Cape, South Africa

Dear Grandaunt Louie,

(I am calling you my grandaunt, because after I had told him everything you had said in Vienna – he was asleep for most of it, remember – Hugh worked out that that was what you were to me. I don't really know what it means except that we are related.)

You see we arrived in Matatiele. I'm so happy because I am where I always felt I was meant to be. I am happy, but I am also very sad. I said "we" just now, but that wasn't the we you might have thought. Hugh died, Louie. He never met my grandmother Nobomi. I wanted very much for him to be with both Nobomis, but he wasn't allowed. He drowned, Louie, like Harry, but the sea did not give him back. They will say it was an accident, but I know the truth was that he just could not go on living. I think he was still ill because of what they did to him in prison. I helped all I could, and there was a doctor in Vienna as well. Sometimes we thought he was healed, but he wasn't. Perhaps we made a mistake, Louie, we went to Harry's grave. I'm sorry. I'm very sorry. Perhaps if it had been Barbara with him and not me. Yes, we worked out in the end how we were connected. I think you already knew that Hugh was the soldier you met on the train, who asked you about the White Cat, which was for Barbara. Barbara is your niece, isn't she, and now she might know about me because Hugh knew he might be going away and he gave her address to a nurse at the hostel where I lived so that they could write and ask her, if I ever needed anything. So I think she will know about me. But I don't know how Hugh knew he would be captured and be in prison for 3 years.

Barbara will not know about Hugh and that he is dead. Perhaps it would be better not to know, do you think?

I have a good thing to tell you too, Louie. But it feels bitter-sweet. (That is something I have learnt from English people, because it is not a Xhosa thing.) I have fallen in love with the doctor from Vienna, who is also English. He was in the Quaker hostel in Vienna where we stayed and he helped us both. Yes, both of us, Louie, because it was not only Hugh whose mind was damaged by what had happened to him. It was me too, because when I was five I saw my mother murdered by my father's family. Don't be upset, Louie, I can feel you crying. There is no need. All is well because the doctor, who is called John came to East London to try to save Hugh, but he could not. But then he brought me to Matatiele, we came a long way on horses to avoid the places which were not safe for a white man and a black girl. But we finally arrived and my grandmother was here. She is still alive, Louie. She is almost completely blind and still lives alone and she knew me in the distance with her eyes which hardly see and shouted – umzukulwana wam – it means – my granddaughter. How did she know, Louie? No-one knew us in this place. She could not see me, but she knew. It was like I was coming home.

We are going to stay here as long as it is safe, but there are rumours of Afrikaner gangs forming and spreading across the higher planes and enforcing the Pass laws. We will have to leave one day and then we will travel into the mountains and cross the border into Basuto – it is British and is not apartheid like South Africa. I will not want to go, but I think that we will be ok, and John and I will carry on the line of Nobomi and Harry.

That is all I can give you, but I am proud of how far I have come. It feels like a huge circle round the world.

I wish you many happy years, dear Grandaunt Louie,

Nobomi

(Louisa Cole – Louie – died 18th December 1976 aged 91)

the end

To have authority is to write your own story and help them to live their own with their beat and their feet and the twistings of meanings into the plaits of time and the resonances of cathedral bells and a whistling in the dark shrouded in fear, and what if they draw from the dreams of early times or far worlds or the whimpering sirens of war, without Physis suffering is just suffering and pain is just pain.

From 'Counterpoint' by Petrŭska Clarkson

Acknowledgements

To acknowledge all those who have contributed, mostly unwittingly, to an author's work would be an impossibility. An author accumulates through observation and interaction, constantly enriched by her or his experience, and all this in some way is present when they sit down to write.

Nevertheless there are those whom I have consulted and who have made more specific contributions from their own area of knowledge and expertise. I am particularly grateful to Alan Brice, a former colleague from therapy and counselling circles who has extensive experience of working with survivors of trauma, in particular those who have been the victims of torture and captivity.

Martin George from Port Elizabeth, now Gqeberha, has continued to be a source of documentation and topical information on that city as well as East London, now eMonti, and Eastbank Cemetery, all of which feature in this book. I am once more indebted to Vumile Kempeni and Polilingua for help with the Xhosa language translations. Ludumo Magwaca has provided assistance as the librarian of The Herald, as has the Cory Library in Grahamstown.

All my ventures are underpinned by the steady support of my wife, Janet, who allowed me to pass over part-complete sections for comment, as well as reading the complete work more than once. The result would have been the poorer without her contributions, for which I am very grateful.

About the author

Simon Cole lives with his wife in the foothills of the Pyrenees Mountains in south-west France. He has been a psychological therapist and trainer for over 35 years. In 2007 he moved from the UK to create a retreat centre in a location which would offer a setting for 'therapeutic release', using the area's natural grandeur as a backdrop for meditation, music, walking and mindfulness.

After many articles in professional journals and online, and books on therapy, meditation and philosophy, "White Cat" was his first venture into a genre of reflective fiction anchored in real lives and events. "Then There Are The Stories" is a sequel and draws on the mystical layer which lies behind and beyond our everyday lives.

book website: www.stillnessinmind.com
email: simon.cole.france@icloud.com